Thomas Edward Amyot

Verses and Ballads

Thomas Edward Amyot

Verses and Ballads

ISBN/EAN: 9783744778770

Printed in Europe, USA, Canada, Australia, Japan

Cover: Foto ©Andreas Hilbeck / pixelio.de

More available books at **www.hansebooks.com**

Verses and Ballads.

BY

THOMAS EDWARD AMYOT, F.R.C.S.,

Of Diss.

NORWICH :

AGAS H. GOOSE, RAMPANT HORSE STREET.

1897.

BIOGRAPHICAL NOTICE.

THOMAS EDWARD AMYOT, the Author of the following poems, prose writings, and drawings, was born in Downing Street, on January 28th, 1817. He was educated at Westminster School; he studied at St. Thomas' Hospital, and afterwards in Berlin and Paris; in 1839 he qualified as Member of the Royal College of Surgeons; and was elected a Fellow in 1866. He became one of the first Scientists in Norfolk, and practised in Diss and the neighbourhood for fifty years, with distinguished ability, winning the highest esteem.

He was a frequent contributor to the Medical Journals, The Journal of Science Gossip, and the local papers. His versatile pen and his

keen sense of humour, are well shown in this
memorial volume.

The family of Amyot is of French Huguenot
descent. Thomas Amyot, great nephew of the
celebrated Jacques Amyot, Bishop of Auxerre,
Translator of Plutarch, and Tutor to Charles
IX. and Henry III. of France, came to
England at the Revocation of the Edict of
Nantes in 1685, and settled at Norwich;
the late Mr. T. E. Amyot was his great-great-
grandson. His father was Thomas Amyot, Esq.,
F.R.S., V.P.S.A., Treasurer of the Society of
Antiquaries, and Private Secretary to the Right
Hon. William Wyndham, Secretary of War in
the "Talents' Administration," whose speeches
he edited with a short but very able account
of his life. He was one of the founders of
the Shakespeare, Percy, and Camden Societies.
Mr. T. E. Amyot's mother was a daughter of
Edward Colman, Esq., Surgeon, of Norwich,
and he married Elizabeth, daughter of the
Rev. Francis Howes, Prebendary of Norwich
Cathedral, the elegant Latin Scholar and translator of Persius, The Odes and Satires of

He was President of the Norwich Chirurgical Society from July, 1878, to July, 1879.

Horace, &c.; she died in July, 1887, leaving a
son and daughter.

In addition to his professional acquirements,
Mr. Amyot was well read in Shakespeare,
and a lover of old literature, and very
fond of music; he wrote many articles on
natural history, chess, and the microscope;
and for the latter invented a "finder" for
minute objects, mentioned in Carpenter's
"Manual of Microscopy." He helped to
originate the Diss Coffee Tavern, and often
gave valuable advice in all sanitary and
philanthropic matters.

A MIXTURE

OF

HARMLESS INGREDIENTS

FOR THE RELIEF OF

MELANCHOLIA, LASSITUDE,

AND THOSE DISORDERS WHICH
ARE APT TO ARISE
FROM ANY

WRONG ACTION ABOUT THE HEART, &c.

"MISCE. FIAT MISTURA."
Doctor's Latin.

THOMAS EDWARD AMYOT.

A BORROWED PREFACE.

" I wish the Reader to take notice that in writing
I have made myself a recreation of a recreation ;
and that it might prove so to him, and not read
dull and tediously, I have in several places mix'd,
not any scurrility, but some innocent, harmless mirth,
of which, if thou be a severe, sour complexion'd man,
then I here disallow thee to be a competent judge ;
for Divines say, ' There are offences given, and
offences not given, but taken.' "

(Izaak Walton).

N the following *mixture* there is no ingredient either of an acrid or bitter nature, and it cannot possibly prove injurious even to persons of the most delicate stomachs or constitution.

The sole act of compounding it has been of incalculable service to one who has suffered much from the terrible disorders mentioned on the title page. Its use in one disease of a distressing character, known by the name of "*perfect idleness*," is quite certain, and the prescriber trusts that it may be of service in many others. Persons, however, labouring under one very irritable and highly *critical* malady, which is apt to show itself in a sort of biliousness often approaching to malignity, every week, month, or quarter, are requested not to meddle with it.

CONTENTS.

ILLUSTRATIONS.

Serious & Religious Pieces.

NATURE.

Lover of Nature and of Nature's God
With thee the guileless hours I would spend:
Where'er thy feet the feather'd grass have trod
By silent stream, in mossy coppice shade,
In daisied mead, or flower-spangled glade
I still have sought thee—harmless, cheerful
    friend!

Far from rude mirth and boist'rous merriment
Be ours the privilege, denied to kings,
To sit unmarked, with hearts whose pure content
Rests high above the reach of worldly things,
Where the broad oak extends his lusty arm,
Or by the brook whose quiet murmurs calm
The anxious spirit, till its plaints subdued
Melt into hymns of pleasing gratitude.

Hark the robins' homely song
Sounds the rustling leaves among,
And seems in sweet and varying note

B

To praise the mighty hand
That tuned its warbling throat.
The lark above its trembling anthem pours
And still mounts high,
As though in fear its grateful lay
Might fall to earth away,
And thinks more nigh 'twill reach his
    Maker's ear.

Look on this pretty weed
Whose leaves still follow in his westward
    course
The glorious Sun,
And yet a dewdrop lingers, as 'twould seem
Weeping to say—
" In some few hours I must die away "
" And no more gaze upon thy holy beam."

From yon high tree the cooing stock dove calls
Repeating still her never-changing note,
And still upon my listening ear it falls
Soft and melodious, breathing sweet content
And tranquil hours in deep seclusion spent ;
No sad complaints her quiet accents know,
To happy minds she breathes no sound of woe,
Save when the rustic tyrant takes her nest,
Or the swift shot has pierced her partner's
    breast.

Here let us rest while yet the glowing ray
With rosy beauties links the azure air,

Here let us linger till the closing day
Brings sleep to troubled hearts and peace to
    anxious care.

Selfish thoughts of worldly pleasure
Leave my fever'd breast awhile,
Bounteous Nature brings a treasure
Free from sorrow, free from guile.
Could the miser now behold
How my bosom heaves with glee,
He would quit his worthless gold
Leave his cares, and follow me:
The pallid student shut his books
And in Nature's perfect page,
In her sweet and various looks,
Read more wonders than an age
Of ceaseless study could bestow
Or the frail wisdom of the world below.
The rising bird at dawn of day
With cheerful note leads on to realms above,
The fading flower at light's decay
Tells of a pangless death in peace and love.
Cease then to sigh
Ye that are bound by sorrow's galling chain ;
Grief comes not nigh
To him who scorns a world of sin and pain,
Who loves to listen to the skylark's strain,
Or when the star at twilight sheds its beam
Faltering and pale
Lingers to hear the plaintive nightingale,

Or by the stream
In happy thought admiring strolls at eve
When every sense
Delighted, strives more keenly to perceive
God's excellence ;
And grieves as midnight shadows close the
skies
And the fair prospect leaves his wond'ring
eyes.

Oh! Man, thy hand hath raised the massive
tower,
The stately vessel owns thy master skill,
The subject brutes confess thy lordly power,
And all things here below obey thy will!

But where is he so skilled in matchless art,
So deep in reason, so mature in power,
That his life's toil could form the meanest part
Of this neglected, unconsidered flower ?

Thou that hast raised the pyramids on high,
In this small shell, behold a work more rare ;
Yon cobweb broken by the captured fly
The weaver's industry can ne'er repair ;

Then let us think ere heedlessly we kill
One glittering insect in its hour of joy,
What excellence ! what care ! what wond'rous
skill !
What passing beauty, we at once destroy.

The meanest creature in its little span
Of happy life, obeys its Maker's will,
The noblest work of God's creation *—Man,
Wise in his errors, doubts and questions still :

Kind Nature speaks in whispers to his heart,
The cold dull heart unheeding turns away,
And knows not that her wisdom could impart
An age of pleasure in a fleeting day.

Spring tells of youth—the Summer bright and
    brief
Of lusty manhood—Autumn's chilling breath
Of tottering age—and Winter's fallen leaf,
Of failing, faltering life, and welcome death.

Yet as the biting winter glides away,
And fresh and green the forests newly wave,
The smiling year reviving seems to say,
" Peace and new life shall wait thee in the grave."

Nov. 1844.

---

* "Il est un Dieu, Les herbes de la vallée et les cèdres de la
montagne le bénissent ; l'insecte bourdonne ses louanges : l'éléphant le
salue au lever du jour; l'oiseau le chante dans le feuillage ; la foudre
fait éclater sa puissance, et l'océan déclare son immensité. L'homme
seul a dit : Il n'y a point de Dieu ! Il n'a donc jamais celui-là, dans ses
infortunes, levé les yeux vers le ciel, ou, dans son bonheur, abaissé ses
regards vers la terre ! La nature est elle si loin de lui qu'il ne l'ait pu
contempler? ou la croit il le simple résultat du hasard ? Mais quel
hasard a pu contraindre une matière désordonnée et rebelle à s'arranger
dans un ordre si parfait."—*Chateaubriand.*

LOVE OF THE WORLD.

(VIEW 1).—A VICE.

Love of the world is darkness of the soul
    The love of God is light:
As in one room we cannot see
Darkness with sunshine reigning,
So in one heart there may not be
World-love and God's in company.
Awake, O man, it is thy false heart feigning,
Masking, and fooling in its Maker's sight,
    Feigning to love things bright
While grovelling in vice and hellish gloom,
Crowning thy foul misdeeds with black deceit
    As eager for thy doom.
Start to the helm while yet it bears control;
Or spread thy flaunting pleasure sheet
And helpless drift along the fatal tide
Urged by the foolish winds and thy heart's pride
    Straight to destruction's shoal.

July, 1859.

LOVE OF THE WORLD.

(VIEW 2).—A VIRTUE.

I love the World,—and wherefore should I not?
Doth the child cast the luscious fruit aside
Because the rind is bitter, or the stone
Contains a tempting poison? Nor will I
Reject God's gift to Man, this beauteous world,
Sweet with the breath of flowers, and glowing
    forth
In rich array of green and golden hues,
While the blue vault re-echoes with the sound
Of Nature's chorus warbled forth by birds
And busy insects, to the rippling brook's
Unceasing symphony. If indeed our vice,
Our faulty passions and corrupt desires,
Will seek but evil—evil can be found,
But blame the world no more; the heart that
    yearns
With love "through Nature up to Nature's God"
Must love, for the great Giver's sake, His Gift,
And leaping boldly from the mists of earth
Will see forth issuing from the wondrous whole
Goodness and Truth and Power; and looking up
To where that Power is best, though dimly seen,
E'en to the glorious canopy of Heaven,
Read in the lettered stars, the Name of God.

March 20th, 1861.

HOPE, THE FLATTERER.

Is Hope a flatterer? yes, if foolish man
Doth blindly lean on her, and dreaming on
Counteth with sighs his wasted hours gone,
And vainly seeketh things unreal to scan.
But meekly ask Religion how to trace
The happiness that leaveth many a mind
In swamps and thorn entangled ground behind,
And make fair reason follow in the chase;
Take thou in present good thy lofty stand,
Attentive mark where Hope's directing hand
Doth point thy way; then bracing every nerve
Let nothing force thee from thy course to swerve:
Thou shalt find strength 'gainst every ill to cope
Nor idly charge with flattery, godly Hope!

1854.

A BEAUTIFUL THOUGHT.

"Suggested during a garden walk, 1845."

Sin is a cobweb—man a stupid fly
  Who blunders in and then find out he's silly.
In vain he seeks some outlet to espy,
  For in the net he lingers will-he-nill-he:
While to escape, his friends with anxious breath
                                        entreat him,
  Down comes the grim old spider Death,
                                        to eat him.

PRESENT AND FUTURE.

With all thy might, O man, with every art
And grateful labour till the ruddy soil.
The earth is thine, the precious gift of God
To work as best thou canst. But the fresh rain
And the great sun with all his generous warmth
Are God's, not thine, nor can thine utmost care
Raise one poor flower to bless thy labour spent
Without their goodly help; nor ought avail
Except by prayer, to gain their fostering power.
They are God's blessings, kept in God's own
    hands.
This present time is thine, 'tis stealing on
Over the silent dial toward the night
" In which no man can work." The present hour
Is thine, God's gift! with every noble art
Suggested by thy heaven inspired brain
Work on to bring it to a happy end.
For like the sunshine and refreshing rain
On the dull soil, will God's high blessing fall
On thy good labour, if thou strivest well,
And bring it to its flower and fruit in heaven.*

Sunday, Sept. 25th, 1870.

* These lines were suggested by the often repeated remark of my
gardener (Mr. Pretty) that he "got them there lettuce plants up very
well," attributing to himself the functions of sun and rain, as well as
those of the mere tiller of the soil. The full meaning of the 16th verse
of the 115th Psalm, which I quote, did not strike me till the fourth
Sunday after they were written, when it occurred in the course of the
evening service (Bible translation).

"The heaven, even the heavens, are the Lord's: but the earth hath
He given to the children of men."

A GRAVE ECHO.

Poor and afflicted, shattered with the strife
The toil and tumult of a suffering life ;
"What canst thou, Death, give to my soul
    depressed ?"
An echo murmurs from the grave—"*deep rest.*"

Feb. 23rd, 1877.

WRITTEN ABOVE AN ERASURE.

Do what we may, a blot is left behind
Where faulty words have soiled the page or mind;
Their drift may be forgotten, yet their stain
In spite of better thoughts will still remain :
For ne'er will Innocence resume the throne
Which once usurping Vice has made her own

A SONNET.

"To the Satirical, the Sarcastic, and Uncharitable."

Like a bad mirror so the selfish mind
  Distorts defects, and every beauty smothers,
And, self-condemned—to all perfection blind
  Shews its own faults where e'er 'twould shew
    another's.

How beautiful is that discerning eye*
  That through the darkness of each human soul
Some bright and priceless jewel can espy,
  Which throws its sacred lustre o'er the whole.

And few indeed are those so lost in sin
  Howe'er by fellow sin condemned, disdained,
But Charity deep-searching finds within
  A pure and noble relic yet unstained.

Folly finds Folly, Vice discovers Vice,
Goodness sees Goodness, e'en through Prejudice.
                1845.

* "Ubi plura, nitent non ego paucis offendar maculis."

HUMAN* VIRTUE.

(So called).

Virtue, so called, in women and in men
Is, in at least nine cases out of ten,
No real and noble effort of the soul
To keep unruly passions in control,
But the mere fruit of accidental station,
Of temp'rament† or cold imagination.
Look then with pity on the child of sin,
Rank noisome weeds in smallest seeds begin,
And pois'nous fruits, that breed the cankering
    worm
From wholesome soil spring up with virtue's
    germ,
Condemn not—curse not—but remember—all -
  Yourselves by some temptation yet may fall.
To save, and not to punish be your care,
And grant the mercy that ye hope to share.

                        1846.

* " Pendant que la paresse et la timidité nous retiennent dans notre devoir, notre vertu a souvent tout l'honneur." (La Rochefoucauld).

† " Virtue and vice ! virtue and vice ! parcel of nonsense !
--State of the stomach--state of the bowels !"
                Sir Anthony Carlisle's Exclamation.

I do not mean in any way to agree with the above theory of Sir Anthony, but quote it for its oddity.

EARLY SPRING.

Fair smiling promise of the infant year
  My heart new throbbing welcomes thee at last,
Sweet bursting buds like dawning hopes appear
  And winter thoughts with winter's snows are
    past.

As the bright streamlet from its sedgy source
  Once more released from icy bondage free
Joyful pursues its mazy-running course
  So my cold breast resumes its liberty.

Through the long frozen earth the hidden seed
  Shoots the green blade rejoicing in the light,
And happy thoughts with glowing lightning's
    speed
  Beam through my bosom chilled in winter's
    night.

The merry birds with ever-varying praise
  Unceasing carol their melodious mirth
Till every sense re-echoing their lays
  Greets thy fair hours and hails thy flowery
    birth.

Fair smiling promise of the youthful year
  Thy glorious sun hath warmed my heart at
    last,
Fair bursting buds like cheering hopes appear
  And wintry sighs with wintry winds are past.

THE LAST WILD FLOWERS OF THE YEAR.

Farewell for the winter fair flowers of the wild
　　Farewell till the bright sun of May;
I have lingered among you as lingers the child,
　　Ye have sweetly my moments of sadness
　　　beguiled,
　　　　And chased my dark sorrows away.

Though many among you may die ere the spring
　　Your sisters will bloom in your stead
As fair as ye are, and their beauty shall bring
　　Some simple admirer their praises to sing,
　　　　Though I, like yourselves, may be dead.

Ye are simple and not in the gorgeous array
　　Of some that are now past and gone;
When they blossomed I sought them, and
　　brushed ye away,
　　But ye bloom for me now in the late autumn
　　　day
　　　　And sweetly smile on me alone.

And so ye have gained on my love as true worth
　　Will conquer when passions decay;
The bright eye may dazzle with fervour or mirth,
　　But the chaste smile of constancy here upon
　　　earth
　　　　Is the beauty that dies not away.

October, 1846.

SONNET.

To a Nightingale.

Sweet bird of night, thou in thy thrilling note
Dost tell the discords of my bygone years.
Who is't has told thee that my secret woes
Well suit thy music, though they mock my tears?
Thy liquid trill, thy long enduring plaint
And mournful cadence bursting into joy,
Throw to the passing winds my varied life,
Love's sweetest pleasure, and its deep alloy.
Straight to my heart thou speakest, while in vain
Sages and Moralists exert their power;
For years of thought could not the solace bring,
That thy dear song affords me in this hour.
Oh let me sing as thou dost, from my heart,
And joys shall fall to me that shall not part.

Signed T. E. A. 18??

A HARVEST SONNET.

"A sower went out to sow his seed."

Sow well with truths the garden of thy mind
And then repose thee like the rustic sower,
Leaving the rest to some superior power,
And in good time the shooting blade thou'lt find.
While yet 'tis young cast out each noisome weed
For though it show full fair above the soil
Thou knowest not how surely it may spoil
By spreading roots beneath, the wholesome seed.

Harvest will come, and thou with thankful care
Thy goodly crop in wisdom's store shalt heap;
Then to the plough, and let the vig'rous share
Bury the stubble-straw securely deep;
That which hath once upheld the healthy grain,
Though dead shall nourish healthy seeds again.

Sept., 1854.

A THOUGHT FROM THE MICROSCOPE.
INFUSORIA.

What is it, I would ask, this atom sees?
That he sees well is evident, for look
He shirks collision with the tiny form
That half transparent to our larger sight
Almost defies the lens's scrutiny.
Yet 'twould be hard to credit that his eye
Can aught discover of myself—he seems
Unconscious of his danger when I place
My finger on the world-drop where he lives.
Oh! what is man or what his vision's range?
How many forms may float between
His littleness and Heaven's Majesty?
May not they swarm more numerous than those
That link his manhood to the smallest worm?
Lord! teach me lowliness, that I may learn
From the small things my feeble eyes discern;
And grant that I with higher things may cope
By the clear vision of a Christian's hope.

4th Feb., 1850.

THE AGNOSTIC.

On the Future.

"Where are you going, Traveller?" "I don't
    know!
Old Time's coat hangs across the only word
I want to see and care for ;
I wish sincerely therefore
They wouldn't make direction posts so low."
    "So low, you say! It seems to me the post
      Points up, and stands at least as high as
      most!"

"What is old Time a'doing!" "I don't know!
He's digging in his shirt sleeves as you see ;
But whether flowerbeds or graves or what
I can't discover, and moreover
I don't much care,—but certes—I don't know!"
    "Don't know! don't care! Is then the work
      of Time
      Nought to a Traveller who's past his
      prime?"

"How came old Time to hang his coat so high?"
"Well I don't know!
But he's so tall—his feet stand neath the granite,
And his head towers up towards yonder planet,
Right through the mists of earth in azure sky."
    "Well then, to hang his coat high after all
    Was nought to wonder at, if he's so tall!"

C

"Is he a safe conductor?" "I don't know!
But *his* way I must go."—
"But if its not a flowerbed—but a grave—
Then Traveller you'll not go?"—
"Alas! I must obey—I'm so short-sighted
Blind and benighted
I cannot choose my way;
So grave or garden-bed, faith, I must go!"
    Stay Traveller, stay and venture not alone
    Along that dismal path.—Alas! he's gone.

Feb. 11*th*, 1889.

NOON-DAY HYMN.

The noon-day sun with glorious light
Almighty Father! greets my sight,
From east to west his blessings fall,
Like thy dear love, bestowed on all.

Lord! let me not in worldly care
Forget Thy praise—forget my prayer,
Nor blinded by the blaze of day
Permit me from Thy paths to stray.

Should selfish dreams invade my breast
And any sinful act suggest
In pity let one thought of Thee
Wake my dull heart, and set it free.

Though godless men my moments grieve
And me with specious arts deceive,
Let me so freely pardon give,
That pardoned I with Thee may live ;

When I the bed of death attend
Or o'er disease and anguish bend
Thy knowledge to my mind reveal
That I may soothe, console, and heal.*

* " La médecine guérit quelquefois; elle soulage souvent, et
console toujours."

C 2

Thou that didst open sightless eyes
And bade the dead—"awake! arise!"
Thou great Physician grant to me
The art a comforter to be.

And when, O Lord, shall come the day
To call me from this earth away,
And when the solemn passing bell
Has sighed to men my last farewell,

Grant that my soul be found in Thee,
From hate, and guile, and envy free,
Made pure and perfect by the love
Shed from its hallowed Home above.

Jan. 5th, 1857.

A SONG OF PRAISE.

" Bless me in this life with but the peace of my conscience, command
of my affections, the love of Thyself, and my dearest friends, and I shall
be happy enough to pity Cæsar."—*Sir Thos. Browne.*

Lord ! in deep sincerity
Praise and thanks I give to Thee.
Since my infant lips could frame
Words to bless and laud Thy name
Thou has filled my heart with song
Tripping upward to my tongue.
Since my eyes could brave the light
Thou hast blessed my raptured sight
       Ever on my view
       Casting glories new,

Now of strange stupendous form,
Smaller now than tiniest worm;
Whether great or small they be
Equal in their majesty,
Equal in proclaiming Thee
Passing good and great to be.
Since mine ears awoke to sound
Thou hast filled the air around
With the music of Thy love,
 Surely earthly things do move
 To a glorious melody,
Which when silent and alone
Mortals hear in dulcet tone,
 Ever—ever—though obscurely
 Sweetly yet and surely
Like some whispering Angel's song
Borne by wavering airs along
 In a ceaseless psalmody;
Now in voice of thunder waking,
Now as rippling water breaking,
Whether loud or sweet or shrill
Telling of Thy goodness still.
Lord, in deep sincerity
Praise and thanks I give to Thee!
Shall I not, O God, rejoice?
Shall I not with grateful voice
Feeble though my humble lays
Living pray, and dying praise?
Living praise, and dying pray
Praying—praising—pass away?

Feb. 9*th*, 1859.

THE MIND'S HORIZON.

" Presume not God to scan."

Oh God, Thou art so great
That in my lowly state
    I cannot know Thee—
If knowing be to see with eye,
To hear with ear, with hand to try,
    I am so far below Thee.

Mine eye doth scan created things,
And to my thoughts Thy greatness brings
    In sun, and moon, and star;
In mountains high, in lovely flowers,
In bounding streams, in tranquil bowers,
    It sees thus far;

But Lord, it cannot scan Thy throne,
Let me its limits gladly own,
    Nor vainly boast,
Through depths above, beneath, around,
To peer, when Thou hast set my bound
    A little mile at most.

I thank Thee that Thy goodness gave
A soul to love, a heart to crave
    Instruction in Thy ways.
To feast with eye, and touch, and ear,
On beauties round me far and near,
    And sing Thy praise.

July, 1888.

OUR NEW CEMETERY.

They are making our beds up the Heywood, love,
Will you walk with me there and see?
There are beds for the young and beds for the old
Beds for the timid and beds for the bold
And beds for you and for me.
They are sparing neither money nor toil
Our beds from damp to free,
But neither damp, nor heat, nor cold
Shall fever the young or chill the old
Who shall take their rest in those blankets of
        soil,
So deep shall their slumber be.
Beds for the aged, beds for the young,
For the babe with the pretty prattling tongue,
For the fair young girl, for her lover so gay,
For the brawler so suddenly snatched away,
For the sick and the sad   for the matron staid,
For rich and for poor is the mattress laid;
Yea, none so hopeless can be found,
But may look for a bed in the Heywood ground.
And who is ready to go to bed?
Not you, nor you, nor I, Sir,
Nor he whose life has in pleasure sped,
Nor the spendthrift, nor the miser;

Nor he who bridleth not his will,
Nor he who wisheth his neighbour ill,
Nor he who swears, nor he who drinks,
Nor the worldly wise, nor the teller of lies,
Nor he who harshly thinks.
There is one—but I know him not yet, dear
    friend,
Who is ready to go to bed,
Who is gentle, holy, kind, and true,
Slow to promise but quick to do,
Thinking no ill, but loving still,
Loving, and sighing that so much sin
Our mortal flesh must dwell within.
Loving and helping, and looking above
Till a hand to the lover is stretched from Love,
To raise him from 'neath the earthly load,
That is laid on his breast in the Heywood road.

Good night, sweet love, be ready I pray
To rise when we're called at the dawn of day.

                     1867.

HEXAMETERS.

Founded on a Prayer for the Sick in the Visitation Service.

Hear us, Almighty God,—all wise and merciful
Saviour!
Thy loving kindness extend to Thy servant
grieved with sickness!
Sanctify to her, O Lord, Thy good paternal
correction!
So, may her weakness give strength to her faith
and zeal to repentance;
So, should it please Thee to bring her to health,
she may live to Thy glory;
So, should she die, through Christ she may rise
to life everlasting!

Sunday Evening, 17th July, 1853.

ON THE DEATH OF A SISTER.

Where is her home?—not here—not with us now,
The placid form lies by us, and the smile
Yet lingers on those lips, which spoke but now
Their messages of love and thankfulness ;
But the fair soul hath flown, and ours the task
To sow the seed corruptible which soon
Will rise in incorruption, and a flower
Shall throw its sacred odour from on high
And we shall call that perfume—" memory !"
Oh ! glorious faculty, that from the past
Dost cull all sweet imperishable bloom,
Leaving sharp thorns and sour asperities
In deepening darkness crumbling day by day,
Fading and falling towards oblivion !
Dear sister, with what gladness shalt thou greet
That kind and holy mother whom we laid
Now five long years ago within the tomb ;
Aye, and our gentle tender-hearted sire !
Ye cannot share our smiles, nor shed our tears,
But oh ! ye sainted three, if heaven allow,
Hover yet near us, and when night has closed
The harsh discordant jarrings of the world,
Whisper in happy dreams all holy thoughts
Of rest and joy to our dull mortal ears ;
Flit lightly round us and with angel wings
Fan the foul mists aside that near us lie
That we may meet in blest eternity.

July 28th, 1853.

THE TWO TEXTS.

M.E.B.

Luke viii. 52.   Timothy ii. 11.

"She is not dead, but sleepeth"—cheering word!
Weep not, she rests from more than daily woes,
From all the world's wild cares in sweet repose
She sleeps! then let no wailing voice be heard.
Yet sleep is death! but she is dead with Him
In Whom to die is life; with Whom to bear
In mortal suffering, is His Throne to share—
Oh, think not death then terrible and grim.
Cast by the sombre mourning, and with songs
Fresh from the thankful heart, exulting praise
The mercy that "to Jesus' name belongs,"
And heavenward still the grateful chorus raise.
Welcome oh Death! thrice welcome, if you bring
With your soul-freeing stroke, no sharper sting.

Oct. 1st, 1854.

LINES.

Written on the fly-leaf of a volume of "*Sacred Poems* by *Henry Vaughan, Silurist,*" which was greatly valued by dear Julia, who died August 18th, 1893.

Sister dear, thy gentle eye
Six short weeks agone did seek
In these pure pages lovingly
All that holy is and meek;

Dreaming as the poet told,
With gilt to beautify thy gold ;
And with colour more refined
To paint the lily of thy mind.
Vain was the dream—from human brain
Thy chastened thoughts could nothing gain.
Viewed in our world's tear-clouded beams
Thy loving soul unsullied seems ;
Seen by the perfect light above,
Spots may be found, but " God is Love."

Sept. 24th, 1893.

—

MY BIRTHDAY ANAGRAM.

January 28th. 1888.

"THERE'S A DIVINITY THAT
28 48 3 5 12 16 1   2 23 11 27 24 33 13 37   34 14 4 53

SHAPES OUR ENDS, ROUGH
38 36 22 42 44 25   10 30 19   20 51 8 31   50 7 15 6 29

HEW THEM HOW WE WILL."
35 49 45   47 17 18 21   39 52 26   43 40   32 46 41 9

A dear God loveth us.   He remains with us.
With Hys help we wither not.

Vale !

28TH JANUARY, 1889.

Seventy-two to-day, O God,
Seventy-two to-day !
Seventy-two, yet above the sod,
Weary and sunk in the earthly clod ;
Seventy-two to-day !
Seventy-two, O Saviour dear ;
Seventy-two, yet strong ;
Waiting a far off voice to hear
Summoning souls from their earthly bier
And their sleep with the earthly throng.

Seventy-two, Most Holy One,
Deigning with me to dwell,
Deigning with me my course to run,
Striving to guide till my course is done,
Guiding from sin and hell.

O God ! O Christ ! O Holy Ghost !
Leave me not here alone ;
Let me not sink beneath the load
I've carried so far along the road
When needing Thy help the most.
Let my heart's grief its sins atone,
And be its prayer—"Thy will be done."

Slightly prospective perhaps.
March 16th, 1889.

GOING! GOING!

"Ye Auction."

Sight growing dim, and hearing a pretence
To hide the failure of that precious sense;
A waning memory, nought that's known worth
    knowing:
Bid up King Death! 'tis "Going, going, going!"
Strength failing, though I strive among the
    throng
To walk with stalwart gait, and pass for strong;
The cemetery walk to see that stone *
Too far, too long—'tis "Going, going, gone!"

Will you, dear friend, or would you if you could
Find up six men to whom I've done some good
To carry this poor frame to that same stone,
When Time the auctioneer cries, "Going, gone?"

King Death's the purchaser Oh foolish King
What good to thee can thy brave purchase
    bring?
An empty case is all! A prize God-wot!
Didst seek my soul? No, 'tis not in the lot.
Far from the heedless world away ' tis flown
Nor hears the hammer fall at "Going, gone!"

* E. A., July 3rd, 1887.

"WARRANTED HOME MADE."

"I will chide no breather in the world but myself: in whom I know most faults."—*As You Like It.*

At many shops—no matter what the trade—
The goods are labelled "Warranted Home Made,"
As if such things wrought with superior care
Were sure to prove too of superior wear.
Well, in my private store—I'm not in trade—
Are goods in plenty "Warranted Home Made";
Heart-wringing cares, and dangers, troubles sore,
So deftly wrought they'll wear for evermore;
Yes all "home made!" and were it not for these
My life were happy and my heart at ease,
For God afflictions has so lightly sent
I know them but for kindly warnings meant;
The bitter lifelong cares I've truly said
Are my own work, yes—"Warranted Home
    Made."

21st *May*, 1890.

THE LORD'S PRAYER.

Oure Father which in Heaven art
　All hallow'd bee Thy name,
Thy Kingdom come, Thy wille be done
　In Heaven and Earthe ye same.
Give us eache daye our daily breade
　And us our sinnes forgive
As we forgive the ills 'gainst us
　Of those with whom we lyve.
Suffer us not, great God, to fall in dread temp-
　　tation's snare,
　But from alle evil us protect
　And shield us with Thy care.
For Thine O Lord the Kingdom is, the Glory and
　the Power
As it hath ever been, is now, and shall bee
　evermore.
Feb. 12th, 1893.

"Use every man after his desert and who shall 'scape
whipping."

Pity I deserve not;
So from Justice swerve not,
Friends, give me none !
God giveth more than men deserve
God from henceforth let me serve.
Pity me, God! "Thy will be done!"
July 16th, 1887.

THE SONGLESS KETTLE.

I've a kettle that never sings.—I hate it—
  And a cat that never purrs :
If you know of a greater grief, Sir, state it,
  No greater to me occurs.

Oh! for a kettle that sings its song,
  For a cat that purrs with a will,
For a laugh and a smile that can care beguile,
  Then life is happiness still.

Jan., 1892.

D

The Last Lines.

D 2

SUNRISE.

The shadows of the restful night are gone,
And tints of rosy grey and tender green
Creep from their holy coverts in the east,
And softly press the parting clouds between.
    Quiet and blissful peace prevail around,
        For men and sin as yet in slumber lie ;
      An early lark upriseth from the ground
        And sings his heavenly praises to the sky.
But lo ! the timid blush of smiling dawn
Bursts into crimson flame. " Parent of good,
Almighty," now the blessèd sun's warm flood
Doth greet us kindly on this glorious morn ;
He rises, rules, and falls *to rise anew ;—*
May I, dear Lord ! his sacred course pursue.

                18th Jan., 1895, 7 *a.m.*

Note.—At 7 a.m. on the morning of the 15th, Tuesday, I did not think I should see another sunrise.

THE OLD DISS CHIMES AGAIN (long silent).

Midnight, 1895.

    In the solemn hour of night
    Stars in heaven shining bright ;
    In the sweet bell voices say—
    "Look on us, 'tis heaven's way."

"Far beyond us in the space,
  Which thy glass can never trace,
  Dwells the God who from above
  Rules thy course with perfect love."

THE TRIUNE.

Jesus, my Saviour dear, night's drawing o'er me,
  Death's gloomy chasm must be near on my way;
Shed Thy fair light on the pathway before me,
  Guide Thou my steps by its comforting ray.

Father Almighty, my God and my Maker,
  Thou who has blest me with mercies untold,
Of Thy dear love an unworthy partaker,
  Me from the power of darkness uphold.

Comforting Spirit, be with me and cheer me,
  Dwell in my heart and preside o'er my soul:
Ever in hellish temptation be near me,
  Ever my thoughts and my actions control.

E'en as I pray the sweet thought of Thy mercies,
  Sweet recollections of undeserved bliss,
From the sad hour of death terror disperses,
  Shedding calm peace o'er the shadows of this.

                              March 8th, 1895.

ENGLISH HEXAMETERS.

THE FIRST PSALM.

Blessed is *he* that hath not walked in the counsel
of sinners

Neither hath stood with the evil, nor sat in the
seat of the scornful ;

But who in keeping the law of his God, hath
ever delighted,

And in *his* law by day and by night, will meditate
alway ;

And he shall be like a tree that hath grown by
the side of the water

That will bring forward in vigour its flower and
fruit in their season,

He shall not wither—and look! whatsoever he
doeth shall prosper.

But it is *not* so with them that walk in the ways
of the wicked ;

For they are like the chaff that is driven abroad
by the tempest.

Therefore the wicked shall not be able to stand
in the judgment,

Neither shall they that sin be found in the
righteous assembly,

For the Lord knoweth the way of the good—but
the wicked shall perish.

Oct. 28*th*, 1846.

THE TWENTY-THIRD PSALM.[*]

Ne'er can my soul know want, for the Mighty
    Lord is my shepherd
Flowery meads shall He give me, and lead to the
    waters of comfort
He shall convert my soul, to His righteous ways,
    for His name's sake
Yea! though I walk in the dark vale of death, no
    evil shall daunt me
For thou art with me, O Lord, Thy rod and staff
    shall support me
Thou shalt prepare a table before me, 'gainst
    them that would wrong me
Thou hast anointed my head with oil, and my
    cup shall be flowing,
Thy loving kindness and mercy shall guide the
    days of my being,
And I will dwell in the House of the Lord, for
    ever and ever.

[*] The 23rd Psalm was my dear mother's great consolation and delight during her last illness. It was read to her a very few hours before her death, and seemed to bring her ease and comfort. On returning from her funeral the above piece was written.

THE CXXXIXth PSALM.

Metre of "Hiawatha."

Thou hast searched me, and known me,
My uprising, my down sitting;
Gracious Lord, Thou understandeth
All my thoughts although afar off.
Thou do'st compass me and watch me
In my path and in my slumbers.
On my tongue no word doth falter
But Thou know'st it altogether.
Thou hast made me with Thy fingers
And hast laid Thy hand upon me.
Too wonderful and lofty
Is such knowledge for my senses;
Whither shall I flee Thy presence?
Whither hide me from Thy spirit?
If I go up into heaven
Thou art there; and if I linger
In the depths of hell I find Thee;
If I take the wings of morning,
Seek the furthest realms of ocean,
Even there Thy hand shall lead me,

And Thy right hand shall uphold me,
If I say—the shades shall hide me
Lo! the night shall glare around me,
Yea, the darkness hides not from Thee
For as day the midnight shineth,
One are light and darkness to Thee.
I am Thine, and Thou didst keep me
In my mother's womb in safety,
I will thank Thee, I will praise Thee
For Thy skill is great and fearful;
I am wonderfully fashioned;
Full of marvel are Thy doings,
  Well my grateful soul doth know it.
Not from Thee was hid my substance
Though beneath the earth in secret
I was fashioned, and my members
One by one were made, and written
In Thy book from the beginning.
Dear to me, Lord, are Thy counsels
Oh! how great the wisdom of them!
If I count them they outnumber
E'en the sand-grains of the ocean!
Sleeping waking, still I'm with Thee.
Thou wilt surely slay the wicked,
Far away then, ye bloodthirsty!
For they idly speak against Thee
And Thy holy name dishonour.
Hate I not, Lord, them that hate Thee,
Grieve I not at their rebellion ?—
Yet, with perfect hate I hate them,

As mine enemies I count them.
Search my heart, Oh God, and know me,
Try my secret thoughts within me,
See if any evil linger
In my soul, and lead me safely
To thy everlasting mansion.

July 27th, 1856.

Ballads.

LOTHBROC THE DANE.

A Legend of the Court of King Edmund at Caistor Castle,
in the Ninth Century.

Lothbroc the Dane,
    King of the sea and land,
    Eagle-eyed and mighty,
    Falcon in hand
    Seeking his sport one day
    Strolled from his friends away,
    Led by his hawk astray.
Lothbroc the Dane,
    King of the land and sea
    Fearless and strong,
    Marks his gyrfalcon
    Swoop to the heronshaw
    Far over ocean.
    Vain is the monarch's lure,
    Down with his quarry
    Into the rolling wave!
    Who shall gyrfalcon save?

Lothbroc the Dane,
    King of the roaring sea,
    Stalwart and reckless he,
    Shall he not save?
    Springs in a fisher's boat,
    Oarless, alone, afloat,
    Sport of the brawling wind,
    Leaving his land behind,
    Lost his gyrfalcon!
    Said I "alone" was he?
    No! for his faithful hound,
    Ulof his matchless hound,
    Shares danger with him.
Lothbroc the Dane
    Wept in his fatherland,
    None know his fate;
    Waves bear him to and fro,
    Winds east and westward blow,
    Sets the red sun,
    Sets in his regal state;
    Sails the moon round and clear
    Sinks in a swarthy bier,
    On the broad watery plains
    Death with fell silence reigns.
Lothbroc the Dane,
    Erst king of boundless wave,
    Now, the mad ocean's slave,
    Helpless and weak,
    Hungered and thirsting, faint,
    None may his anguish paint,

None words of comfort speak;
Only his faithful hound
With him to suffer.
Where his broad kingdom now?
Hemmed in by stern and prow;
Where his sleek courtiers?
One only can he see,
Shaggy his coat may be,
But staunch and brave is he,
And his heart's steadfast;
Ne'er by great Lothbroc's throne
When fortune kindly shone
Crouched a more trusty one.
Never by Monarch's side
When left by Fortune's tide,
Flouted by all beside,
Stood a more true one.

Lothbroc the royal Dane
Leave we in fevered rest
On the wild ocean's breast,
Of wind and wave the jest;
Ulof his faithful hound
Watching his sleeping.
Sets the red scorching sun:
Sails the moon bright and clear,
Sinks in a watery bier.
Death with black silence reigns
On the broad foaming plains.
Storms shout and roar,
Waves beat the shore.

Edmund of gentle mien
  Noble and just I ween,
  King of East Angles,
  Holds Court in Caistor's towers,
  Rides in the morning hours
  Down where the sluggish Yare
  Woos the rough ocean.
  Marks the wild sea-birds' flight,
  Dolphins all gleaming bright
  In the sweet morning light,
  Few that attend him;
  Few serfs await his call;
  Loving and loved by all,
  Friend both to great and small,
  Love is all powerful,
  Love will defend him.
  Why stands the King enthralled?
  What hath his sense appalled?
  Why scans his eye the beach
  Far as the sight can reach?
  Calls be to Humbert—
  "Humbert—dear trusty friend,
  Quickly assistance send
  To yon poor fisher.
  See how his shattered boat
  Half stranded, half afloat
  Strikes the rough shingle.
  If he be living found,
  Throw my warm cloak around,
  Gently attend him.

See that my faithful men
All succour lend him.
Warm his cold form, and then
Straightway to Caistor towers
Tenderly send him.
Poor fisher though he be
That he be cared for see,
As though a nation's weal
Hung on his welfare."
Edmund of gentle mien
Noble and kind I ween,
King of East-Angles,
Bends o'er the prostrate form
Shattered by wind and storm,
Drenched by the breaking wave.
Whose is the life they save?
One shaggy hound,
Shaggy and strong of limb
Leaves not his master;
Leaves not caressing him,
Friends in disaster.
What tells the signet ring?
Lothbroc! the Danish King!
Lothbroc's the life they save
From the wild ocean wave!
Edmund of guileless mien
Guileless and true I ween,
King of East-Angles.
Lothbroc the stout and brave,
Snatched from a watery grave,

E

Noble of heart,
Kings of two mighty powers
Sit in fair Caistor's towers,
Sworn friends for ever ;
What shall that "ever" be?
God of Eternity,
What shall that "ever" be?
Wait, and the answer see!
Edmund the King,
True as pure heart can be
Generous and free,
"Build me a ship of might
One that may plough the wave,
Skim o'er the surf so light,
One that may tempest brave.
One that may bear a King
Safe to his fatherland ;
Where his sons sorrowing
Weep on the strand.
Meanwhile let mirth be crowned,
Story and song go round,
Jest and good will abound,
Sweet harp and trumpet sound,
Care in the cup be drowned."
"Health to our Royal Guest
Long may fair peace entwine
Lothbroc's with Edmund's line
Loving and blest!
Bring the trained coursers
Mighty and free and fair,

Fit kingly freights to bear."
Falcon and hound are there,
Hunters' shouts rend the air.

Bern, the King's Falconer,
    Swarthy and stout of limb
    Dark-browed and silent.
    None flouts a jest at him :
    Silent, and scowling round
    Hates he, with hate profound,
    Strangers on Anglian ground ;
    Jealous of Danish King,
    Vexed at his sway at Court,
    Vexed at his skill in sport,
    Stands he low murmuring ;
    Pressed lip, and darkling eye
    Vengefully burning.

Lothbroc the Dane,
    Where has the monarch strayed?
    Why his return delayed?
    Went he not out to-day
    Bern, the King's Falconer
    Bearing him company?
    To the dark woods away,
    Scan the white sea-bord,
    Search every crest and bay ;
    Where can the Monarch stay ?
    Ulof, brave Lothbroc's hound.
    Shaggy his coat may be
    But true and brave is he,

Leaves not his master;
Trusty in glittering court,
Trusty and strong in sport,
True in disaster;
Where stays the gallant hound?
Sweep the broad country round
Find *him*, and Lothbroc's found.
Three weary days are gone,
Comes Ulof all alone;
Takes at the throne his stand,
Licks royal Edmund's hand.
One stands beside the king
Swarthy and strong of limb,
Dark-browed and silent.
Growls the brave hound,
Deep mouthed with thundering sound.
Outspeaks great Edmund—
"Bern,—prithee tell me why
Glares the hound at thee
Bare fanged with flashing eye?
Gentle is he as child
Harmless and mild?"
"Nay, Liege, I know not why,
But ever savagely
Greets he my fond caress.
Treacherous I deem the hound
Savage and faithless.
Pleased it your royal mind
Straightway a thong I'd find,
Hanged the Dane-cur should be

On some nigh-standing tree."
"Not so" the King replied,
" Ulof shall be our guide,
Ho there! the search renew
Scour the thick forest through!
Quakes my firm heart with dread,
Lothbroc alive—or dead
Straight must be found."
Quick from fair Caistor's tower
Rides forth a lordly band
Some to the ocean sand
Some to the river.
One only lags behind,
Dark-browed and dark in mind,
Yet his lips quiver.
Edmund and few beside,
Ulof their trusty guide,
To a dark copse away ;
Little their footsteps stray
Eastward or westward.
Sick pale the sun had been
Now bloody red I ween
Sinks he to rest.
Why bays the gallant hound ?
Why starts the steed around
Stiff limbed and tremblingly ?
"Bern—to the front,
Search well yon tangled fern.
Seems to us, Bern,
Backward is not thy wont

When soars the hern."
Mark the King's Falconer,
Swarthy and strong of limb,
Dark-browed and silent,
Now pale as dying child
Faltering his gait.
"What ails thee—Bern?
No woman's heart hast thou:
Why dost thou tremble now?
Why pales thy sweating brow?
Forward I say
Down with the tangled fern
Trodden it seems to us
As though in deadly strife
Life had sought life."
Oh! Edmund, brave and good
Now quails thy generous blood
What greets thy sight?
Lothbroc thou see'st once more,
Pale-lipped and bathed in gore,
Blood-stained the ferny floor.
Leaps thy true heart?
Edmund, thy cheek is white,
Faltering thy sight;
'Tis but an instant— now
Flushes the Kingly brow,
Flashes the wrathful eye,
Firm the command.
"Seize ye the murderer Bern,
Bind him both foot and hand,

Bear him away,
Set him alone afloat
Oarless in Lothbroc's boat
Sport for the scorching sun
Sport for the chilling dew
Sport for the raging storm
Sport for the wild sea mew.
Anguish and pain
Seize on his recreant form,
So let him die."
Lothbroc the Dane,
Once King of land and sea
Mighty and free;
Beats his bold heart no more,
Pale cheek besprinkled o'er
Purpled with royal gore.
Wailing and woe
Fill Caistor's stately tower:
Sadly and slow
From the wide portals go
Mourners in lengthened row,
Warriors of might and power
Ride forth with saddened brow;
Pomp, and black royalty
Dust in the dust to lie.

Moans the great ocean
Sighs the sad Northern wind
Groaning like one bereft,
Widowed and mourning left

Restless in motion.
Idly along the tide
One fisher-boat
Oarless, afloat,
Seems like a ghost to glide.
Bern, the King's Falconer
Stout limbed—but feeble now,
Swollen with blistered brow,
In the sun's glare,
In the night's baneful air.
Rages the sea,
Wildly to heaven tossed
Now in hell's caverns lost
Rides the boat drearily.
Dreams the King's Falconer!
Hears in the seabird's note
Lothbroc with severed throat
Gurgling wild curses out—
In the wind's moan
Hears Lothbroc's flying groan;
Sees in the scudding rack
Bloodhounds on deadly track!
Ulof, with eager howl,
Frights his black soul.
Sinks he in heart and breath
Fears life and death.

Darkly, as through a glass,
See we the ways of God,
Darkly His judgments pass
Ill understood.

Else why to Danish land
Drifts the unguided boat
Steered by no human hand
Oarless, afloat?
On the wild beach
Crowds watch the coming wave,
Eager to save,
Eager in speech.
"Yes, 'tis the missing craft!
Can the foul blistered thing
Fast bound with many a cord,
Can that be Denmark's King?
That our lost lord?
Search fore and aft.
No King, but lives he yet?
Numbed by long cold and wet!
All succour send him,
Kindly attend him."

Bern, the King's Falconer,
    Roused from half death, and free,
    Base and malignant he
    Seeks the King's palace.
    Ingwar and Hubba bold
    Hear his false story told,
    How that in malice
    Lothbroc their royal sire
    Fell 'neath the murderous brand
    Grasped by vile Edmund's hand
    Who in his ire,

When *he*, their faithful slave
Strove the King's life to save
Straightway had bound him,
Cast him in Lothbroc's boat,
Helpless, alone, afloat
E'en as they found him.
Hubba and Ingwar
Thirsting for vengeful war
Swear ne'er to sleep again
Till they reach Anglia's shore!
Till bloody Edmund's slain
Feast they no more.

Leave we to future rhyme
How the base Falconer's crime
Wrought England's bitter woe;
Turned England's friend to foe,
Brought in its cursed train
Fell wars and endless pain.

March 4th, 1870.

EGLESDENE.*

The first part of the following Ballad relates to the defeat of the Danes by Alfred, at Okeley in Somersetshire (A.D. 878); the second part to the fall and martyrdom of Edmund, at Eglesdene or Hoxne in Suffolk (A.D. 870.) It was immediately before the battle of Okeley that Alfred entered the Danish camp in the disguise of a harper, and discovered the weak points of the enemy's position.

"All glory to our gallant king,
　　And to his warrior train,
Who upon Okeley's purple field
　　Have crush'd the haughty Dane.

"Drowned in accursed pagan blood
　　Their hell-born ravens lie,†
While waved once more in Freedom's breath
　　Our Saxon colours fly.

"Hail to each gallant patriot hand
　　That glows with foeman's gore!
All hail to him who triumphs yet,
　　And him who fights no more!

* Now Hoxne.
† The raven was the famous Danish standard, and was regarded by the soldiers with superstitious awe. It was supposed to clap its wings before victory, and to hang its head at approaching defeat.

"The royal harp with dulcet sound
    Beguiled the sottish Dane;
The royal sword spread death around,
    And swept him from the plain.

"The blood that many a Saxon heart
    Hath shed on Saxon land
Shall rise again in tenfold might,
    To blast th' invading band.

"This speck upon the ocean's breast,
    This little isle of ours,
Shall yet be Freedom's sacred seat,
    And laugh at tyrant powers.

"And unborn warriors to their sons*
    And grandsons shall recite,
How Hubba and how Ingwar fell
    'Neath good king Alfred's might.

"All glory to our gallant king,
    In whose victorious hand
The minstrel chord and patriot sword
    Have freed our Fatherland!"

Thus sung an ancient warrior bard
    On that right glorious day,
When heaven had nerved the Saxon's arm,
    And checked the pagan's sway.

* Both Hubba and Ingwar were killed in the battle of Okeley.

Attentive to the glowing theme
  The mighty Alfred stood;
Then turning to the aged man
  Spoke him in kindly mood :—

"Well hast thou sung, my ancient friend,
  Yet, when thou sing'st again,
Sing that the Lord did edge our sword,
  Else had our strength been vain.

"And lest our pride should overflow,
  And swell presumption's sea,
By claiming more than man may claim
  In fair humility—

"Sing me, I pray, the mournful tale
  Of sacred Edmund's death,
When God vouchsafed to take his soul,
  Though pagans took his breath:

"How, though his cause was great and good,
  'Gainst countless ills he strove,
And how, through woes and misery,
  He found his Saviour's love.

" Then if thy tongue, by glory fired,
  Would frame a worthier lay,
Praise Him whose strength our souls inspired
  To deeds of might this day."

To mournful strain the bard again
   Attuned his trembling lyre,
And tempered well with solemn swell
   The patriot's lofty fire.

"To God alone, the Infinite,
   Be all our praises given;
Though fortune bless or woes distress,
   Praised be the hand of Heaven.

"From darkest seeds, that evil seem
   To man's imperfect eyes,
Unnumbered blessings spring around,
   Unlooked-for mercies rise.

"In sad defeat or victory
   The ruling power is God;
So let us raise the hymn of praise,
   Or kiss the chastening rod.

"And shame be mine, most Christian king,
   That in my graceless lay
My vaunting pride to God denied
   The glories of this day."

Lost in conflicting thoughts awhile
   The aged minstrel stood;
Then bending low his humbled brow,
   Began in mournful mood—

"Oh woe the day, the bitter day,
　When Heaven's supreme decree
To ravening pagan's ruthless sway
　Bowed low the Christian's knee.

"When, all outnumbered by the Dane,
　From Thetford's* castled seat
The Saxons fought their blood-stained way
　To Framlingham's retreat.

"And long, by kingly Edmund led,
　In those majestic towers
Defied the swarthy Ingwar,
　And Hubba's savage powers.

"Till, fiercer still than foeman's hate,
　More keen than foeman's brand,
The ghastly sword of famine fell,
　And thinned their gallant band."

"'Now yield thee, Edmund!'" cried the Dane.
　"'Not so,'" the king replied,
"'But bid your knaves prepare to stem
　A Saxon torrent's tide;

"'For ne'er will Edmund sheath his sword,
　Or plead with downcast eye,
While one brave heart obeys his word,
　While Danish ravens fly.

---

* "From Thetford," on the authority of the Anglo-Saxon Chronicle ;
but some say that Edmund fled from Dunwich.

" Though fate may yield this earthen case *
    To wear the pagan's chain,
Yet there's a soul that burns within
    Which thou canst ne'er restrain.

" There is a King of kings above,
    Whose standard still I hold,
And ne'er will Edmund yield its grasp
    To king of earthly mould.

" Down with the drawbridge ! carve a road
    Through this unhallowed band ;
Bathe with their hearts' distempered blood
    Our fever-stricken land ' "

" He said, and with the lightning's speed
    The gallant host shot forth :
The Danes ran east, the Danes ran west,
    The Danes ran south and north.

" And well, I trow, the Saxon bow
    Sent forth its deadly shaft.
And deeply drank the Saxon steel
    Its crimson-flowing draught.

" Yet soon the Pagans formed again ;
    And as the night drew near,
Like troops of Satan's hounds, swept on
    And pressed the Saxon rear.

---

  * The substance of Edmund's reply is given by Lydgate, and in
M. Casnewe's " Life of St. Edmund."

" Unto the woods of Eglesdene *
　　Our soldiers fought their way,
And purchased not a foot of ground
　　But what their blood did pay.

"And there, though torn by famine's fang,
　　They sought to make a stand,
And once again to beard the Dane
　　And free their Fatherland.

" But all too weak, both man and horse,
　　To face the pagan host;
And many a gallant Christian corse
　　To Christ gave back its ghost.

"And the brave king exhausted fell
　　Beside a gentle stream,†
And laid his sacred head beneath
　　A bridge's spanning beam.

"And there, concealed from foeman's eye,
　　Secure he might have staid,
But that a luckless chance, I ween,
　　His whereabout betrayed.

---

* Eglesdene or Hoxne—
　　" Oxen hate the toun ther the body felle."—
　　　　　　　　　　　　　　Hearne's *Langtoft*.
† The little "Gold-brook," crossed by a foot bridge which is still
called " Gold-spur Bridge," is a tributary of the Waveney.

F

"Serene the pallid moonbeam shone
    Upon that fatal night,
And dewy showers on sleeping flowers
    Gleamed with a diamond light;

" When o'er that bridge there chanced to pass
    A rustic wedding band,
That paused in listless idleness
    Upon the grassy strand.

"The glittering spurs of Edmund caught
    A moonbeam's envious ray,
And to the gaping crowd revealed
    The nook wherein he lay.

"The trait'rous clowns in cursed greed
    Their secret basely sold,
And, Judas-like, damnation bought
    In blood-besprinkled gold.

"(And ne'er since then hath bridegroom ta'en*
    The Gold-spur bridge's way;
But bitterly the bride hath rued
    The deed of blood that day.)

---

* The curse of St. Edmund still retains sufficient force to induce all newly-married parties, who have occasion to cross the Gold-brook, to escape its influence by passing over a foot-bridge about a quarter of a mile out of the direct road.

Like hell-begotten blood-hounds then
  The pagans scoured the ground,
And, guided by a traitor hand,
  The good Saint Edmund found.

" They lashed him to a sturdy oak,
  In cruel jesting mood;
Their arrows pierced his sacred sides,
  And drew his noble blood.

"With stripes and scoffs and impious jests
  They mocked his body's pain,
Who, like the Master whom he served,
  Reviléd not again.

"But when he felt his life-blood flow,
  With heaving bosom then
He prayed the Lord to turn their hearts,
  And make them Christian men.

"Thus died great Edmund, Martyr, Saint; *
  Yet ere his spirit fled,
In savage zeal fierce Ingwar's steel
  Smote off his kingly head.

---

* " He attired him to bataile with folk that he had,
    But this cursed Danes so grete oste ay lad,
    That Edmunde was taken and slayne at the last,
    Full far fro the body lay was the hede kast."
                                    Hearne's *Langtoft*.

F 2

" How that the body guarded was
By wolf less fierce than they.*
Till holy monks the treasure found,
It boots me not to say.

" But well hast thou, victorious king,
With God's high blessing, been
The avenger of great Edmund's death
In bloody Eglesdene."

---

* The old legend goes on to say that Edmund's followers found the
body, but could nowhere discover the head, until a voice cried " Here,
here, here !" and guided them to a part of the thicket, where they found
it guarded by a wolf. It united to the neck, leaving only a mark like a
"purpil threde." The wolf accompanied the body to its resting-place,
and then retired to the woods "without shewing any fierceness." The
bones of a wolf are said to have been found enclosed in a stone coffin
while repairing the old "Norman" tower at Bury St. Edmund's, in
1848. On the same day, 11th September, 1848, the fine old tree known
as St. Edmund's oak, fell down, during perfectly still weather, at Hoxne,
and on cutting up the trunk an iron arrow-head was found embedded in
the wood near its centre. The curiosity is now in the possession of
Sir Edward Kerrison, Bart. Singularly enough, at this very time,
September, 1848, the curious little wooden church at Greensted in Essex
was undergoing repair, and its split oak trunks were, for the first time
since their erection in 1013, lying on the ground. The connection of
this fact with the history of Saint Edmund is this— In 1010, during the
reign of Ethelred "the Unready," the Danes ravaged the country, and
the bones of the Saint were removed for safety to London. After three
years they were carried back to Bedrichesworthe (Bury St. Edmund's),
and on the way were deposited in a "wooden chapel," the nave of this
ancient church. See a most interesting account of Greensted Church,
lately published by the Rev. P. W. Ray.

MARGERY GRIMES.*

Ding Dong
    For evensong
The bell's fair summons is borne along
As the wild wind wills it faint or strong;
For funeral knell or for young bride's hopes.
The village folks say—
    (They be wits in their way)
"They ring 'coz old Billy's a pullin' the ropes."

Old Margery Grimes is sick in her bed,
And she's dying and dying, but not yet dead;
A hocusy pocusy, conjuring rocusy,
Charm-working hag and a wicked old crone she is
Spiteful and blasphemous,---that we all own
    she is,

---

* This is the foundation on which the accompanying tale is built—
Mrs. James Borrett, of Scole, had seen better days, and although when
I knew her keeping a small 'dame's' school, was a fairly educated, and
I should say a sober-minded and truthful woman. She told me that
some years ago she sat by the bedside of an old woman (whom I have
called Margery Grimes) of evil reputation, who was dying. Her
cottage was near the tower of the church, and the bells were chiming for
evening service. After watching by her for many hours, her breathing,
which had been noisy, suddenly ceased. She got up to look at her, but
was dreadfully alarmed by the old woman starting up and bursting into
a hideous fit of wild laughter, shouting out that she'd "been up o'the
steeple and frightened old Billy rarely!" At the same moment the bells
ceased with a clash, and Billy the sexton, rushed out of the tower into
the street, swearing that "Madge Grimes had been up into the belfry
and frightened him." The old woman really died a few minutes after
this.

Drying the cows with her evil eye,
And blasting the crops with her grammarie,
Helped by Grimalkin, her swivel-eyed cat,
Bony and gruesome, and black as your hat,
The devil's half brother—no doubt about that.—
But she's dying and dying and not yet dead
And she mutters her oaths on her truckle bed
In a tumble down chamber with sulphurous air,
A rat-burrowed wainscot—a rickety chair,
Neither you, Sir, nor I would have cared to be
    there.
Yet one good old soul,—'tis the schoolmaster's wife
Sits watching the close of her flickering life,
And she knits, and she knits by the glimmering
    light
Of a single rush-candle kept well out of sight,
Socks for the poor and a nice little vest
For tiny Bet Smith with the delicate chest,
And hour by hour she marks the hard breath
And the measured throat-rattles that end but
    with death.
        But 'tis Ding, Dong.
        For evensong
The bells fair summons is wafted along,
Whether for death or for wedding-day hopes
As the mad wind pleases it faint or strong,
And the village folks say
(They be wits in their way)
"That they ring 'coz old Billy's a pullin' the
    ropes."

—The good wife leaves her rickety chair
And eyes the old crone with womanly care,
For her breast heaves fitfully slow and fast
And the rattles and breath fight for first and last;
While her thin lips mutter the curses of hell
Which I may not write and I dare not tell,
And her fire-eyed cat improves his place
The better to gloat on the dying grimace
Of his bad old mistress's leathery face,
Just as if he'd a share in the life or the death
Of the beldam's soul and her faltering breath.
Still! all still!—save the wild wind's roar
And the rats working hard twixt ceiling and
floor,
And the rattles have ceased—to be heard no
more.
The good wife closes the glazing eyes
And covers the face from the bluebottle flies,—
But she swoons outright
In ghastly fright—
For as if awoke from a devilish dream
The crone starts up with a long wild scream,
And a hideous laugh that drowns the din
Of the blast without, and the rats within—
"Ha Ha, Ha Ha! Ho Ho, Ho Ho!
"The dead ride fast on the to and fro',
"Grimalkin and I on a broom travel fairly,
"We've been unawares up the old tower stairs
"And frightened old Billy rarely!"

Ding Dong—Smash!
Did ever you hear such a crash?
Is Billy gone silly to make such a clash?
No, Billy runs quick down the old church stair
And his face is as pale as his snow white hair,
He falls in a swoon, and with vacant stare
When he comes to himself is ready to swear
That old Madge Grimes and her damnable cat
Two devils incarnate,—no doubt about that,
Had flown on a broom up the bell chamber stair
While he tolled his ding dong, and affrighted
   him there.
And from that dread hour neither money nor
   power
Could bring him again to that old church tower.
He hadn't a mind, so he could not go out of it,
Had it otherwise been he'd have done so, no
   doubt of it.
Little remains to tell or to write
But that Madge and her cat both vanished that
   night,
While her hut by spontaneous combustion
   ignited
And the smoke every tree in the neighbourhood
   blighted.
Some say that old Madge and her swivel-eyed
   friend,
Who shot horns and a tail with an arrow-shaped
   end,
In the midst of the flames was observed to ascend

On a broom, then describing a circle or two
   In the air
   The bad pair
Sank down to the earth—and then tumbled right
   through!
   Ding Dong
   For evensong
The bells keep it up for ever so long,
And the village folks say
(They be wits to this day)
That whether for death or for wedding-day hopes
They ring 'coz old Billy's *son's* pullin' the ropes.

My friend Dr. Pollen, botanical lecturer,
Man of real science and no mere conjecturer,
Examined the spot
Where once stood the drear cot,
And said, when last summer he came down to
   stay by us,
That nothing would grow there but *devils-bit-
scabious.*
The small *Myosurus** which people call 'rat's-tail,'
A *Valerian* potent in swelling a cat's tail,
And a kind of *Tremella* too dreadful to utter
But pretty well known as the famed Witch's-
   butter.
He professed too to fear neither goblin nor sprite.
And declared in the belfry he'd pass one whole
   night;

   * The Spaniards call Myosurus –' *Cola de Raton.*'

For that spirits, by weak folks esteemed
'diabolical'
Less mischief performed than the kind—'alco-
holical.'
But the squall of a cat and the low moaning
wind
As he went there, induced him to alter his mind.
Though he said—and 'tis right his own reason to
mention,
"Other business required his immediate attention."

March 2nd, 1882.

A LEGEND OF AIX LA CHAPELLE.

Oh! Aix, I ween, is as fair to see
As any town in Germanie
But strange is the story I'm going to tell
Of the Church it is christened from "Aix la
Chapelle."
Whence came all its splendour? O! listen and
hear!
When Charlemagne's bones lay incased in their
bier
In a snug little chapel he'd built for himself,
Great Otho the third tried to gather the pelf
In order to build up a beautiful choir
As fair as the Emperor's shade could desire.
But useless his efforts, in vain did he send
His satin-cream-laid, and post paid without end
With a one-penny stamp to the folks he thought
willing
And prayed by the return of post "one little
shilling!"
All, all was in vain, for the hard-hearted scamps
Never answered his letters and captured his
stamps.
In vain did he hang money boxes around
On every blank space of the walls that he found,

He never saw aught when he opened the lid
But a spider, a bit of a pipe, and a quid,
Which some nasty devil by way of a dole,
Or a small contribution, had poked through the
  hole.
The town council sat, and the town council
  mourned
For ever as wise as they met they adjourned,
Though each of the members was sure his
  advice
If followed, would raise all the cash in a trice.
The chairman he spoke and the chairman he
  yawned
But never one novel idea on him dawned,
Though the thanks of the meeting still greeted
  him there
For the great satisfaction he gave in the chair.
All useless their counsels and vain their debate
Till one night a councilman rather irate
Said that all their grand schemes would be left
  in the lurch
If the Devil himself didn't pay for the church . . .
Rap a tap, rap a tap, rap a tap, tat a tat,
And rap a tap, bang, rap a tat, rap a tat,
Not one of the councilmen e'er heard before
Such a terrible tapping as now shook the door.
The chairman looked wild, and the council
  aghast
As they though every rap a tap must be the last,
Till after the lapse of a minute, walked in

A gentleman well dressed, lame, swarthy, and
   thin.
The assembly at first, with ill-grace at the best
Gave a kind of salute to the unbidden guest,
But he with such accent and pure nonchalance
As proved him well known to the élite of France
Spoke thus—" Mes amis, ne vous dérangez point
" De vos vains conseils, moi, j'ai été temoin,
" Je me hâte, la richesse de ma bourse vous offrir
" Pour faire votre église digne de tous vos
   désirs."
With an air and a grace on the table he threw
A bag full of ducats all shining and new,
Saying "when you want more you need only
   apply—
" But there's one *slight* condition I ask, by the
   bye."
Diable! quoth one, a condition! let's hear:
The Deuce! cried a Hoch-wohl geborener Herr,
Who'd deny a condition, whate'er it may be
And forfeit the glittering heaps that we see?
" 'Tis only just this" said their guest with a grin,
" Everyone has his taste; if I've mine, 'tis no sin.
The first, male or female, young, old, fat, or fine,
That enters the church, when complete, must be
   mine!"
Sacré nom! Donnervetter! odds bobs! ventre
   bleu!
What odd interjections about the room flew,
As each of the council, with hair straight on end

Gazed in fear and dismay at his newly made
 friend.
Having somewhat recovered their first conster-
 nation
They entered at once into grave consultation,
And at last they agree, 'tis their safest
 position
To pocket the gold and accept the condition.
" We'll contrive that some twopenny soul should
 go first
A beggar, a thief, a sacristan at worst ;
But in order our well contrived project to save
Let each keep the secret as still as the grave."
" Not a word " said they all, not a word, not a
 breath,
Let our secret be kept with the silence of death.
Yet 'tis true, though how 'twas I am puzzled to
 say
But their wives knew the whole ere the following
 day !
You'll allow this was strange, but a far stranger
 thing
As a lover of fact, to your notice I bring :
It is this, ere the night had again spread her veil
Not a soul in the city but knew the whole tale.
Well, in process of time " la chapelle " was
 complete
And crowds of admirers paraded the street.
The priests at the doors begged of each to step
 through

But the constant reply was—"Monsieur, après
  vous!"
Such a row for precedence was never I ween
In the salons of fashion or royalty seen,
But the donkey race rule was in every one's
  mind,
'Twas not, who shall go foremost; but who stay
  behind.
The case became desperate; there stood the fine
  church
With its altars and candlesticks left in the lurch
And again the town council tried hard to suggest
In the awkward emergency, what course was best.
'Twas in vain—till one night when all Aix was
  asleep
Or rather when eastward the morn 'gan to peep
The chairman, with force he'd have spared to a
  dumb thing,
Slapped his wife, and cried out, "Gad! I've hit
  upon something!
A great ugly wolf, my dear wife, do you see,
Was entrapped near the spot where the station's
  to be;
And shoot me, but we'll try human victims to
  save
By driving his wolfship bang into the nave."
The plan was approved of by all, and once more
The crowd had collected before the church door;
A gaunt famished wolf was brought up, while
  within

Crouched the dragon, Beelzebub, swarthy and
    thin,
With wide open jaws and with teeth of cast steel
He lay wagging his tail at the thoughts of his
    meal
And stretching his throat like a hideous gulf—
Hark! a shout! Who's the victim? A nasty
    old wolf!
Poor Nick was bamboozled, he sputtered and
    spit,
And tried to eject the unsavoury bit,
But in vain,—so enraged, he rushed out might
    and main
And kicked the church door till he kicked it in
    twain,
Then knowing his fury could nothing avail,
He paused but to tie a huge knot in his tail
That he might not forget to have beds warmed in
    hell
For all future guests out of Aix la Chapelle.

A wolf and a fir-cone, in bronze at the gate
Stand attesting the truth of the tale I relate,
The first, as a portrait in gratitude taken
By the Aix la Chapellians for saving their bacon
The latter, a thing tasteless, hard, dry, and
    sticky
Which figures the morsel that choked poor old
    Nicky.

And now for a moral, for e'en from this story
I hope to be able to lay one before ye—
Don't believe when some folks make a show of
    their cash
In presenting stained windows, and cutting a
    dash
In the church building line, that their motives
    are sure
In point of religion and zeal to be pure :
What a feasting of tenants, and bunning of
    schools,
What splendid donations, and balls for the Poles,
What clothing of niggers, we see every day
Where the end of the "Patrons" is merely
    display.
Believe me, dear reader, I would not detract
From the merit so due to true charity's act,
Such thoughts be far from me, I wish but to say,
In the hour when hopes in this world pass away
The kind heart that shrinks from applause will
    beat lightest
And that bushel-hid candles burn sometimes the
    brightest.

July 17th, 1849.

FRAU RICHERMONDT.

A Tale of Cologne—in fact, the original " Ode de Cologne,"
but not by J. M. Farina.

In the Grand Parade at Cologne the traveller is struck with the
strange position of the wooden effigies of two grey horses which are
peering out of the upper window of a high and ancient house. The
following is the legend connected with them, as related to me by a
commissionaire on the spot.

The doctor he sat by Frau Richermondt's side
With his anti-epidemical,
But the fearful disease permitted no ease
And baffled each drug and chemical.

Quite vainly he tries his pounded crabs' eyes *
And his powder'd Theban mummy,
And his syrup of lice, and his toasted mice,
And his balsams fœtid and gummy;

And useless the flesh of the viper fresh
And his pigeon alive cut in two,
Which he thinks it is meet to apply to her feet,
And his hedgehog elixir won't do.

So he rose from his chair, with a solemn air
And thrice he shook his head,
And he said with a sigh (that was all my eye)
" Frau Richermondt is dead ! "

* The dainties here enumerated were all in use as medicines about a
hundred years since. Others equally choice might be mentioned--
spirits of skulls and toads among the number.

" I've tried my skill with potion and pill,
I've done for her all I believe is best,
All things that I've heard, however absurd,
I've tried, but—*vita brevis est.*

"I've given her ice, and lice, and mice,
And spice, and rice, and brandy;
I've given her mummy and nasty things gummy,
Whichever might turn up handy,

"I've wrapped her so neat in a well-wetted sheet,
From her heels slap over her head,
And more I could mention, but vain my attention—
Frau Richermondt is dead."

Snug under the Dom in a costly tomb
Frau Richermondt is laid,
The glare of the day has past away,
And a mass for her soul has been said.

'Tis deep midnight when the noisome sprite
Plays leapfrog over the grave,
What man then is here who seems not to fear
The wrath of the dead to brave?

He kneels him down by the sculptured stone
The heap with a crowbar turning,
Of the faltering moon he's missed the light,
But his bull's-eye 's dimly burning.

'Twas the sexton, and few were the things he
  spoke
And he breathed not a word of sorrow;
But he said—"if I cabbage that ring to night
I shall be all the richer to-morrow!"

He tugged at the finger on which did linger
The gold-encircled stone,
Then drew from his pocket a knife to unlock it
By paring the flesh from the bone.

But scarce was the blade to the cold skin laid
Ere—horror of horrors to tell!
The death-cold claw grasped the sexton's paw,
And the knife from his clutches fell.

Well! what did he do? just as I, sir, or you
Would have done in a similar plight,
In a swoon he fell down on the cold clammy
  stone
And in falling banged out his light.

Frau Richermondt rose—not so dead, you'll
  suppose
As she seemed when she was buried—
Hit the sexton a blow on the shins with his crow
And into the city she hurried.

She found her own house all as still as a mouse,
Save the cats' serenade on the tiles,
And she shouted aloud as she stood in her
  shroud
"What the deuce are ye arter, Giles?

"How dare ye to snore while I stand at the door
All shaking and shivering and freezing?
My clothing is light for this time of night
And 'tis anything but pleasing."

"How came you, I say, to stow me away
Without being sure I was dead?
Oh—no doubt you'd a plan to provide—you bad
    man,
Another Frau R. instead."

Herr Richermondt moaned, and Herr Richer-
    mondt groaned,
And he uttered a hideous scream.
For facing him there, stood a ghastly nightmare
Intruding herself on his dream.

And the devil sat squat in her saddle, I wot
And bellowed out might and main,
"Lieber Herr, I have brought you the treasure
    you thought
You never should see again.

"Hark! your wife's at the door; don't you hear
    the uproar?
Wake up then, and strike a light."
Herr Richermondt rose, rubbed his eyes and his
    nose
And sat himself bolt upright.

No devil was there, but a chill of despair
Crept over his trembling frame
As he heard the sweet voice of his wedding day
    choice
Calling his "once loved name."

The epithets queer were harsh to hear
With which it was linked, alas!
She called him a blundering son of a gun
And a muddle-headed ass.

Was't a ghost or a Banshee, that horrible fancy
The wraithe that at dying folks' window knocks
Or dreadfuller far, was it real Mrs. R.
As he groped in the dark for his tinder box?

Yet believe it he couldn't, and didn't, and wouldn't,
But he seized on his matches in ire,
One hundred and two of the lot wouldn't do
But the hundred and third caught fire.

No Bryants and Mays in those far away days
Excited the popular "vox"
As they tooled it along in the four-in-hand
    throng,—
"Only striking indeed on the " *box*." *

He reached the last stair in the chill damp air,
He opened the door in a fright,
His *bonnet de nuit* seemed as frightened as he,
For its tassel stood bolt upright.

---

  * One of the great firm dashes away in Rotten Row and the Parks with other great but more mischievous match makers.

For there in the gloom, come fresh come from
    the tomb,
Frau Richermondt stood in her shroud ;
But her spouse kept afar, with the door just ajar
And breathing again, said aloud :

" Oh ! goblin immortal, avaunt from my portal
Back, back to your region so drear !
For my wife I have lost her, thou ghostly im-
    postor,
She's *there*—so she can't be *here*!"

In vain her entreaties, in vain were her sighs,
In vain were her words, rough or kind,
For preparing to shut up the door in a pet
Thus her husband delivered his mind.

" I'll no more believe that my missus can leave
Her snug quiet grave in the Dom,
Or raise the big stones that are laid o'er her
    bones
To come plaguing her husband at home,

"Than my horses could stray from their corn
    and their hay,
Through the double-locked stable door,
And marching in pairs up the back kitchen stairs
Make their way to the uppermost floor."

The words were scarce spoke, when a wild
    neighing broke
On the silence of the night,
At the window I ween, two horses were seen
In the glimmering pale moonlight.

(I don't know, I declare, how the horses came
    there,
But certify this I *will*,
That the story can't be a complete l.i.e.
For their effigies stand there still.)

Herr Richermondt saw, and he crossed himself
    o'er
From the tip of his nose to his chest,
Then seizing his wife in her newly found life
He clasped her once more to his breast.

Not a soul that I know has e'er witnessed I trow,
Nor the oldest inhabitant seen a
Connubial meeting so warm in its greeting
Since Edwin and Angelina.

Oct. 25th, 1849.

"ISAAC WALTON" ON THE FISHERIES EXHIBITION.

(Reported by "A MEDIUM.")

TO THE EDITOR OF THE NORWICH MERCURY.

Norwich, April 18th, 1881.

Dear Sir,—I claim your courtesy, being a well-known medium,

To ask you, on your readers to inflict my Psycho-tedium

In an attractive vision's form, the while I was entranced—

And for the time beyond dull earth, to spirit-land advanced;

Where sat good Isaac Walton, as of old benign and jocular,

And peering through a spy-glass of a kind that's called binocular;

Near him his friend Venator stood, and Auceps too was there;

Each praised, as erst on Tottenham Hill, the Water, Earth, and Air.

Venator sang "Tantivy," and, with joy that knew no bounds,

Described a burst of wondrous pace with old
    Tom Moody's hounds:
While Anceps praised the tuneful birds that to
    the 'shame of art'
Send from their instrumental throats such songs
    as touch the heart.
As first the lark, who cheers herself, and those
    who hear her song,
Quitting the earth and mounting high the golden
    clouds among;
Anon she groweth mute and drops to the dull
    earth amain.
Which but for sheer necessity she would not
    touch again,
And then the lady Nightingale breathing such
    music out
As leadeth thoughtful men the end of miracles to
    doubt.
Who that has heard her sweet descants, the
    trillings high and deep,
The doubling of her heavenly voice through
    midnight's darkness sweep,
But feels himself as lifted up above this murky
    sphere
And whispering thus in undertones to God's all-
    listening ear
"What music, mighty Lord, hast thou reserved
    for saints in heaven
Who to the sinful men of earth such glorious
    strains has given?"

He ceased, and asked good Isaac if he'd kindly
let them know
What by his glasses he discerned through earth's
grey mists below?
To whom Piscator—" Friends who once loved in
the purling stream
To hook the perch and savage pike, bright trout
or slimy bream,
Who loved in mood contemplative to watch the
dancing float
In the black depths of forest lake, or castle-
guarded moat;
And you who on the stormy wave 'mid the mad
ocean's strife,
Poor fisher, lost for hearth and home thy oft
imperilled life;
Come near and hear of wondrous things which
through my glasses I
In that fair city of the East, Old Norwich can
espy."
The sprites of ancient Glaucus and of good Sir
Henry Wotton,
Of Doctors Donne and Whittaker, and lively
Charlie Cotton,
One too, a stately abbess,* long removed from
earthly thrall,
Who loved the honest angler's art, obeyed
Piscator's call:

* Dame Juliana Berners.

And thus the ladye praised the craft in voice
most musical—
   " Atte least the Angler hath his holsom walke
   And mery at his ease doeth hungry growe
   With savoure sweete of meade and daintie
     floures.
   Heareth melodyous harmony of birdes,
   Seeth white swannes, and cotes with callowe
     brood;
   Whyche seemeth me farre better than the
     noyse
   Of houndes, and blastes of horns, and cryes
     of foules,
   That Hunters, dogges, and Fawkeners can
     make.
   And if the Angler taketh fyshe, than he
   No mery soule alive can merrier be." •
Well said, fair dame, quoth Isaac, now attend
while I disclose
What honour on our gentle art old Norwich
town bestows.
I see through my binocular a gallant cavalcade
With people making holiday in colours bright
arrayed,
Banners are waving in the streets and dashing
soldiers throng
The crowded thoroughfare, through which a car-
riage rolls along:

---

* "Treatyse of Fyfshynge with an Angle."—Emprynted by Wynkyn
de Worde, 1496.

In it a lovely lady sits, whose kindly smile makes
glad
Rough country folks, and cheers the heart of
many a sailor lad,
Who from the coast has made his way, with
some perception dim,
That ladies fair may even care for such poor
chaps as him.*
Beside her sits her royal spouse—a prince who
never spares
What prince can do - and much he can, to lighten
poor men's cares.
To-day he comes to aid the cause of those brave
sons of toil
Who on the deep uncertain sea undaunted seek
their spoil,
Risking for wife and children's sake, in storm
and seething foam,
Their lives, nor deem their lot severe, and
cheerly dream of home.
But now the goal is reached, and while the lordly
trumpets blow,
The Royal guests and all the crowd enter the
spacious show,
Boats, nets, and trawls, and fishing craft, and all
that man contrives
To reap the harvest of the seas, or rescue human
lives

---

* Sailors' grammar.

From watery graves; bright glittering fish in
  roomy tanks I ween,
And baby salmon burst the egg, and join the
  busy scene.
The Princess and her Princely spouse, well-
  pleased and pleasing all,
At the good Mayor's request repair to famed St.
  Andrew's Hall,
Where a right royal déjeuner the hungry guests
  awaits,
And the great organ's notes are drowned by
  music of the plates.

But now a marvel I behold : scarce have the
  guests retired
From the great show, ere all the fish by one
  strong impulse fired,
Leap to the largest tank and round its depths in
  glittering row,
E'en as in ancient Norwich guilds, in long pro-
  cession go,
Six stalwart eels for whifflers, and a dogfish
  acting Snap,
While herrings helter-skelter fly, nor like the
  game mayhap,
Asserting and with reason, that his play is rather
  rough,
As he gobbles of their party rather more than
  quantum suff.

At length they settle to a feast, great Neptune
takes the chair,

(I'm not prepared to tell you, if you ask how he
came there?)

Sweet lob-worms à la maitre d'hôtel, gentles in
matelote,

With hookless flies to tempt the trout, and frog-
lets cold and hot,

And many another dainty dish—full duty done
to each,

When Neptune waves his trident thrice, and
makes this telling speech.

"Fishes and friends from every sea, from every
tarn and lake,

From every stream that to my realm doth
contribution make,

I fill my cup,* most kindly lent by courteous
Mr. Reeve

From the Museum's topmost shelf, and by your
gracious leave

Will give the health of Homo-Man, to whom we
owe the treat

Of being here this day—not where we're
eaten—but to eat;

'Tis true you deemed him once your foe, but
on consideration

He did but save you from the curse of over-
population.

＋ A huge fossil sponge called " Neptune's Cup."

Doth he not pass great Acts to check our river's
    foul pollution,
Preserving you from fell disease, from filth,
    and destitution ?
Doth he not during spawning time forbid illicit
    sport,
Protecting you from thieves that soon would
    bring your race to nought ?
Look round and see the training troughs and
    ova hatching tanks
Wherein your progeny are reared, and give to
    Homo thanks.
I own there's more to wish for, Friends to anti-
    vivi-section
Should to my noble friend the cod 'gainst
    crimping urge protection,
And though with some slight show of truth
    they urge that ancient use
Tempers the eels to skinning,—yet it looks like
    an abuse;
I well might say a word or two 'gainst cruel
    salmon spears,
Let's hope their use will very soon be discon-
    tinued"—(Cheers!)
An oyster whispering Neptune prayed *his* hard-
    ships might be heard,
But Neptune, loving oysters much, refused to say
    one word.
Some slight molluscan discontent, a laugh, and
    shouts ironic,

Threatened for some few minutes a *dénoûement*
inharmonic;
For then a lobster wished to speak 'gainst being
boiled alive,
And crabs and shrimps obstreperous disturbed
the watery hive;
But Neptune, equal to the task, with smiles and
softest sawder,   .
Concluded thus his speech and quelled all
symptoms of disorder:
"Take him for all in all, sweet friends, Homo's a
noble beast,
So with his health in three times three we'll
crown this joyous feast!"
Having no hands to clap, all wag their sym-
pathetic tails,
And Sturgeon, king of fishes sings, "God bless
the Prince of Whales!!!"

    *   *   *   *   *   *

Here broke my trance, and once again on *terra
firma* fixed,
I sign myself "Your Medium," just now *a little
mixed.*

H

Ɦeroic.

--- ---

God give us peace—or honor, if in war
Our bloodless swords must from their scabbards
    leap,
If friend and foe in cold and ghastly heap
Must pave the way for Triumph's crimson car.
But oh! if honor be dear England's gain,
Bought with the life of many a gallant heart,
Grant it be pure, and shew no tarnished part
Where lust or cruelty have left their stain.
Nerve the rough soldier's arm—but let his ear
Be open to the orphan's piteous cry,
Let his fierce eye yet soften at the tear
Shed by the widow of an enemy.
So may success attend our country's might
And God be praised—for God with us shall fight.

SONG AND CHORUS.

Written for the Diss " Haven of Success Lodge of Oddfellows."

Oh! welcome to the seaman's ear
  When tempests shake the main
The shout of "Land"—the land he thought
  He ne'er should see again.
So welcome is the friendly call,
  When stormy griefs oppress
When tears in ceaseless torrents fall,
    To the *Haven of Success.*
        Then where's the man that will not join
          With willing voice to bless
        The toast of Friendship, Love, and Truth,
          And the *Haven of Success.*

The roaring winds may hoarsely blow,
  And fiercely rage the storm,
No power to chill the heart they know
  With sacred kindness warm,
The coldest breast shall thankful prove
  And moved to joy confess
The noble worth of *brothers'* love
  In the *Haven of Success.*
        Then where's the man that will not join
          With willing voice to bless
        The toast of Friendship, Love, and Truth
          And the *Haven of Success.*

Let knaves upbraid us *—fools believe –
  Our *duty* still remains
To help the friendless and relieve
  The sufferer of his pains.
With Honor faithful to our helm,
  No skies shall us distress
We'll safely sail with favouring gale
  To the *Haven of Success.*
     Then where's the man that will not join
      With willing voice to bless
     The toast of Friendship, Love, and Truth
     And the *Haven of Success.*

The following verse was added for the Jubilee of the
Lodge in May 30th, 1894.

Just half a hundred years are gone,
  Yes, fifty years, since we
Sailed out from port,—and now we've won
  Our happy Jubilee;
And friends are gone and friends have come,
  Young heads have turned to grey,
Yet sit we here and sing with cheer
  Our lusty roundelay—
     May God, our Country, and our Queen,
      With health and plenty bless,
     And Friendship, Love, and Truth be seen
     In the *Haven of Success.*

---

* At its commencement Odd Fellowship had to encounter a good
deal of opposition and ridicule.

FATHERLAND.

Another version of " What is the German's Fatherland ? "

Which is the German's fatherland ?
Bohemian land ? Bavarian land ?
Or where yon faltering servile band
Would kiss the Czar's despotic hand ?
Oh tell me not that this can be
That land of heroes and of chivalry.
Oh Austria ! to all allied,
For ever strong on stronger side,
Thou ramping calf in lion's hide,
Vain land of tyranny and pride ;
It cannot be, it cannot be
But Honour's call is nought to thee.

Which is the Frenchman's fatherland ?
Is't where a group of tremblers stand ?
Where timid princes hold command,
And sink in shame their native land ?
Oh, no! oh, no ! its ancient name
Was ever linked with deeds of fame.
And still its flag by glory fanned
Floats nobly towards the hostile land,
And gallant hearts beneath it, seek
To crush th' oppressor of the weak ;
This then must be—this then must be
The land of Frenchmen and of chivalry.

Which is the Briton's fatherland ?
Is't Scottish land, or Irish land ?
Or where the cliffs of England stand
While roaring billows sweep her strand ?
Oh no ! the Briton's home must be
The sea-girt shores of all the three.
Oh ! Britain, since thy glorious form
Has ruled the wave and braved the storm
Full many a conflict hast thou seen,
Yet ever true thy sons have been.
This then must be—this then must be
The Briton's fatherland so free.

INKERMANN.

To the air "Krieger's Abschied."

Daylight is passed—the dark Crimean night
In chilly pall enshrouds the dead and dying.
Fitful is seen by cannon's lurid light
Where friend and foe in fever'd sleep are lying ;
Yet one bright vision cheers the soldier's heart,
A well-loved form his dreaming thoughts dis-
    cover,
One, now so far away, in angel accents seems to
    say,
" We'll part no more—for stormy war is over "

Murky and slow the gloomy shadows break,
A call to arms dispels the warrior's slumbers.
Rifle and gun the sullen echoes wake,
And foes sweep on in mist-enclouded numbers.
Yet one fond thought makes firm the soldier's
    arm,
And cheers his heart while dangers round him
    hover,
One, who is far away, in gentle accents seems to
    say,
" We'll part no more when stormy war is over."

Dauntless and well the hardy Britons fought,
And gallant Frenchmen shared the battle's glory,
Dearly the victor's laurel crown was bought,
Its leaves with many a hero's life-blood gory ;
But far away, in sorrow and in care
A gentle girl laments her soldier lover,
Now bent in silent prayer—bowed down by chill
    despair,
She sinks to rest ere stormy war is over.

Dec. 20th, 1854.

Humorous.

OLEUM JECORIS ASELLI.

An Epistle to my Sister
At the Rectory of Fritton,
Written very shortly after
I arose from the perusal of the *Song of Hiawatha.*

Do you ask me why this letter,
Why this long and dreary letter?
Why this waste of ink and paper?
Scribbleabos—ink and paper?
 I would answer, I would tell you
 'Tis about a Codfish liver;
 Yes, the liver of a Codfish,
 Bullysprat, the king of Codfish.
 Would you wish to know the wherefore
 The *Pourquoi* the why and wherefore
 You are plagued about a Codfish?
 I would answer, I would tell you

In the oil of codfish liver
Dwells the Manito of healing,
Gitche Sanitas the healer,
He the mighty health restorer.
Do you ask me who discovered
In his dark and greasy dwelling,
In the oily Codfish liver
Gitche Sanitas, the healer?
I would tell you, I would answer
In the days of Pterodactyl,
In the wondrous days of darkness,
In the days of flying lizards,
In the Oolitic era
Ere was born the huge Dinornis
Ere the Mastodon was thought of,
When the fish were mighty rulers,
And when none were there to fry them,
Lived King Bullysprat the Codfish;
And a secret burned within him
Which he dared divulge to no one
Lest his life should pay the forfeit.
Till one day confiding strictly
In a Lobster's great discretion
(Quite forgetting for the moment
That within his dusky cranium
Lodged a lady who could hear him
Who'd be sure to let the cat out)
Thus he told his fatal secret
" Hear me, Sable Crust the Lobster,
Hear me, sagest of crustaceans,

And be silent! In the future,
In the dim and distant future,
In the kingdom of Postpona,
In the land of the Hereafter
Shall a queer and savage creature
Having two legs and no feathers,
Nor a tail to wag with pleasure
Nor to droop in grief and anguish,
On the earth set up his wigwam.
He shall suffer from diseases
And shall dig the earth for physic,
For Argentum, Plumbum, Zincum,
And Hydrargyrum and Cuprum.
He shall cull the forest flowers,
Make infusions and decoctions,
Tinctures, pills and lotions, ointments,
Beastly nasty draughts and mixtures.
He shall try the Hydropathics,
Mesmerists, and crazed professors
Of infinitesimal nonsense,
Nor shall fail in every effort;
For the cure of all his ailments
Lies just where he'd least expect it,
In my fat and oily liver,
In my horrid filthy liver,
In the liver of the Codfish,
Gitche Bullysprat, the Codfish!"

And the Lobster took his Davy
He'd be silent as an oyster,

Yet before a week was over,
"Boil me scarlet," quoth the babbler,
Babbling Sable Crust, the Lobster,
He the villainous deceiver,
Good in nothing but a salad,
He the tittle-tattling babbler
With the lady in his noddle,*
"Boil me scarlet, but I'll venture
Just to tell my friend the Herring!"
And the Herring, Yarmouth Bloater,
Hated Bullysprat the Codfish,
For he'd gobbled up his father,
And his mother, and his brother,
And what's worst of all, his sweetheart,
So he thought 'twould serve him rightly
To inform his friend the Turbot.
And the Turbot told the Porpoise
(Very like a Whale was Porpoise).
And the Porpoise told the Sunfish,
And the Sunfish told the Mullet.
And the Mullet told the Whiting,

---

* When I wrote this I certainly thought that everybody knew all
about the lady in the lobster's head, for from my youth up I have
thought the search for her hardly second to the eating of the rest of the
dainty crustacean. But I find I am mistaken, and that very few people
know even of her existence. Let me tell them how to find her. Take a
boiled lobster—or, better still, give me one—and in the so-called head I
shall find a membranous bag (the stomach). I slit it open and behold a
beautiful lady dressed in ivory and coral, reposing in a magnificent ivory
and coral chair. You keep the lady and I have the remainder as my
perquisite. The chair and the lady are really gastric teeth.

And the Whiting told the Haddock,
And the Haddock told the Sturgeon,
And the Sturgeon took his T out
And became a learned surgeon.
    (Fish as odd as he have taken
    Out a Kill-and-Cure diploma
    By a method quite as simple).
Well he knew the vast importance
Of the secret whispered to him
As a point of Therapeutics,
But as no man lived to tell it to
He told it unto no man.
Unto an Egg he told it
And the Egg brought forth a Starfish,
Asterias the Starfish,
And the Starfish hatched a Mollusk,
And the Mollusk hatched a Lizard,
And the Lizard hatched a Dodo,
And the Dodo dropped an ovum
In the depth of a volcano.
The volcano shook and trembled
And lo! a Mouse came from it;
And the Mouse begat a Weasel,
And the Weasel bred an Otter,
And the Otter an Opossum,
And from him a grinning Monkey,
And the Monkey a Gorilla.
And Gorilla reared an Aztec,
Yes, a wild and savage Aztec,
Yes, a biped without feathers,

And the Aztec reared a Bushman
And the Bushman is our brother,*
And the brother of the author
Of the "Vestiges" you've heard of,
Who would tell you, if you asked him,
That the story of his being,
The development of Bushmen,
Is the same that I have told you.

Thus the Biped without feathers
Came to know the fatal secret,
And he made a line of catgut
Of the strong unyielding catgut
Pussyviscera the catgut
And a hook he baited deftly
With a patty made of oysters,
Yes, a tempting oyster patty.
In a punt he sat and angled
For Great Bullysprat, the Codfish,
Crying "Take my bait, oh Codfish,
Gitche Bullysprat, the Codfish!"

* *A Note of Development.*
Pace Lyell, Pace Darwin,
Pace "Vestiges," and others,
Whether Orthos, or Agnostics;
But if ultimate perfection
Be development of spirit
At expense of flesh and matter,
May not much despised Amœba
Of whose spirit no one knoweth
But whose flesh is next to nothing—
Be the outcome of the Aztec?
Not the Aztec of Amœba.

But the Codfish only answered,
"See you further first, you blockhead,
What a fool you are to sit there!"
Seven days he sat a fishing
With his mighty line of catgut,
And the tempting oyster patty
Ever fishing, ever crying
"Take my bait, oh! mighty Codfish,
Gitche Bullysprat the Codfish."

Till the Codfish, waxing angry,
Called aloud to the Sea Serpent,
Whom he thought to make a catspaw
Like the monkey with the chestnuts.
"Break the lubber's line, Kenabeek,
Mighty seven-league Kenabeek!"
But Kenabeek only answered,
"If you want it broken—break it!"
And sailed off to see the Yankees.

Seven weeks the patient biped,
Fished for Bullysprat, the Codfish;
Ever fishing, ever crying,
"Give me of thy oil, oh Codfish,
All thy oil, oh greasy Codfish."
And the Codfish muttered gruffly,
"You're a modest chap for certain,
Very modest your request is,
But I'd rather not, I thank you."
And lay sulking at the bottom;

Till one day he pricked his dorsal
Fin with Holdemfast, the Fish-hook.
Moved to savage indignation
Then he seized the oyster patty,
Yes! the patty made of oysters ;
And he pulled the line to break it,
But King Bullysprat was done for.

Yet from morning until sundown,
And from sundown until morning,
From dawn to latest midnight,
And 'twas pull devil and pull baker,
For three weary weeks together,
Till great Bullysprat, the Codfish,
Weak with struggling, fainting, failing,
Fell a victim to the biped.

Great Apollo, God of Physic,
Gitche Manito of Physic,
Looking down from high Olympus
Saw the struggle of the Codfish,
Of Great Bullysprat the Codfish,
With his featherless opponent.
Like a very hot potato
Then he dropped the grand sonata
He was just about composing,
And slid down upon a rainbow
Like a great celestial spider ;
Straight he hung the mighty Biped

In his fishing line of catgut,
Killed the Codfish, cut him open,
Put his liver in his pocket,
Saying—" Folks of the dark ages
Are not worth so rare a medicine,
So I'll save it for the people
Of the days of steam and rail-roads,
Telephones and light electric,
And I'll cure the later sages
Of the rheumatiz and phthisic.
Thus I name this mighty nostrum,
Oleum Jecoris Asclli."
Oil of Bullysprat, the Codfish!
By Apollo's letters *patent*.
Please observe the stamp—Beware, too,
Of all spurious imitations.

ENVOI.

I have got your oil, oh sister!
The Norwegian oil, oh sister!
At just six and six the gallon.
'Tis the same, I'm pretty certain
As De Jongh, the arch imposter,
Sells at most unheard of prices
To the gaping British public.
Easy gulled, the English public.
Shall I send it by the railway,
By the Eastern Counties Railway,

I

By the railway, the delayer,
The eternal parcel-loser,
Puff and blow, the Eastern Railway?
Or shall I wait till either
Of our legalizing brethren,
They, the Manitos of Mischief,
With their azure bags of wampum,
Take a trip by rail to Fritton,
Or will Sable-coat, the White-throat,
He, the mighty Fritton Rector,
Call and take it at the station?
Will you tell me, will you answer?

November, 1855.

SONG OF "ANACHARIS ALSINASTRUM."

Oh my leaves are three together, oblong, serru-
  late, obtuse,
Yet wherever I present myself I'm subject to
  abuse
Though an unprotected female for my husband,
  who's a Yankee,
Hasn't yet appeared in England—though he's
  pretty well I thank ye.
'Tis hard, I think, that folks should hate me like
  the rats and vermin,
I 'spect because my bifid spathe's much longer
  than my germen;

My stem is slim, my pretty whorls like Oregon
    annexed,
Yet they seek to cast a stigma on my stigma so
    deflexed ;
My sepals are diaphanous, incurved, and pink
    externally,
But with all my charms you Britishers detest
    me most infernally.
I've travelled from Dunse Castle, what a dunce
    was I to go there !
Through Leicestershire to Swainsthorpe, on the
    dreary brink of nowhere ;
And to give you folks in England here of enter-
    prise a notion,
I'll next choke up the channels of the vast
    Atlantic ocean,
To stop each British bull-dog, Spanish don, and
    Gallic poodle
From crossing o'er to laugh and jeer at glorious
    Yankee doodle.

Feb. 4th, 1854.

To the unbotanical reader the following note to the song above
may be useful :—The Anacharis or Udora is a waterweed
unknown until lately in England, and which has probably been
accidentally imported from America with timber, &c. However its
sudden appearance here is to be accounted for, it is doubtless a very
troublesome visitor, as by its prodigious power of increase and its
unhappy knack of catching hold of everything with its countless hooks
it has already choked up to a very serious extent the midland canals, the
river Cam, and other important streams. Dunse Castle, near Berwick-
on-Tweed, was one of the first localities in which it appeared, and it has
lately started up in a most unaccountable manner in a small pond quite
unconnected with any navigable river at Swainsthorpe, a small village
about three miles south of Norwich. The female plant only is known in
this country; and the injury to navigation, &c., is already immense

THE PENITENTS.

A True Story.

In days when Georgius Tertius wore the crown
A worthy surgeon* lived in Norwich town
Who an apprentice† or assistant had,
A reckless, idle, merry-hearted lad,
Whose careless ways brought troubles rather
    faster
Than was convenient to his lord and master.
An evil habit—now discreetly broken
Of uttering oaths with every sentence spoken
Reigned in those days; and much it grieved the
    Leech
That such a senseless vice should taint the speech
Of man and master both,—for well he knew it
The *age* of *one* should lead him to eschew it;—
The *youth* of t'other;—so with contrite heart
In which his 'prentice claimed to bear a part
They thus agreed -for every uttered oath
Sixpence to pay—and binding on them both!

---

  * My grandfather, Edward Colman, Esq., Surgeon to the N. & N.
Hospital.

  † The late distinguished surgeon and excellent fellow, Bransby
Cooper, Esq.

Pleased with the good resolve so wise and sound
The Doctor started on his daily round,
But short, alas! his triumph—for 'twas o'er
E'en as he entered his first patient's door
With "How's your mistress? how's your mistress,
   nurse?
Better I hope?"—"Better! good lord, she's
   worse
With spasms 'orrible and pains excrunching
As if on arsenic pies she'd been a lunching,
And all along o' that there imp of evil
You calls your 'prentice—*we* the Doctor's devil,
Who's sent a *pison* lotion—though it say
"A wine glassful or so three times a day!"
Boiling with rage the Doctor homeward flew
Kicked at the surgery door, and bursting through
Banged it behind him with an echoing slam,
And yelled aloud a most sonorous "damn!"
—"That's sixpence, Sir," his worthy 'prentice
   said,
I'll chalk it on the wall till it is paid;"
"No d—n it, Sir, I'm serious."—"That 's one
   shilling,
I'll mark that too—that is unless you're willing
To pay at once." Then came a fearful oath
Which to describe both pen and ink are loth,
While cool as cucumber that 'prentice stood.
"Just eighteen pence," he said out burst a flood
Which the recording angel hovering near
Let's hope has blotted with a kindly tear.

" Two shillings, half a crown, three, three and
    six "—
The raging Doctor now at nothing sticks—
The 'prentice scoring shillings into pounds,
For greed and rage know neither check nor
    bounds.
And so the sum increased from much to more
Till both exhausted swooned upon the floor!

Next Sunday that apprentice wore his best coat,
A dandy tie, and satin-flowered waistcoat,
A watch and seals—folks wondered at his dash
And where that whipper-snapper got his cash!

29th May, 1890.

THE ADVANTAGE OF SCIENCE.

The ruling passion, &c.

The learned Cuvier went down below
Where French philosophers are *said* to go; *
Howe'er that be, Old Nick delighted much
At getting such a *savant* in his clutch ;
So donning all authority and ease,
"Cuvier," said he, "go down upon your knees!"
"I'll see you further first," great Cuvier cried.
"Well then, I'll eat you up!" Old Nick replied.
"You *eat* me up," said Cuvier, with a smile
Taking a knowing glance at him the while,
" *You* eat me up! now from such trash deliver us.
Horns and a cloven hoof ! why, Sir, you're gram-
     iniverous."

T. E. A., *Oct.*, 1846.

---

* The joke is not mine, but is so good I thought it worth versifying.
  A certain French philosopher wrote as follows :—" I, if I exist, leave my soul, if I have a soul, to God, if there be a God."

PROFESSOR TADPOLE.

A ditch! only a ditch! not a lake, nor a mere,
nor even a pond! no, only a ditch--a long broad
ditch by a quiet road-side; but a very deep
ditch, and now in early April, as indeed at
all other times of the year, full of such clear,
pure water that it was a treat to the eye to
look into its crystal depth--a treat something
akin to looking up into the blue vault of
heaven (to compare great things with small)
and like *it* begetting a sort of dreaminess and
a thrill of indescribable happiness in the gazer;
though I well know that there be gazers *and*
gazers, so you need not quote Wordsworth to me
to show that some folks would have passed my
ditch and seen "nothing more" in it than his
rustic saw in the "primrose by the river's brim."
What *I* saw in it was this—a wealth of bright
green foliage, the starwort and the young leaves
of the delicate water-ranunculus, long streamers
of rich mosses, and vast patches of soft
confervæ, with here and there a budding mass
of ulva; and all set off to perfection by the
red-brown carpet of last autumn's leaves
which floored its depths. But animal life
was scarce; only a few minute water snails,

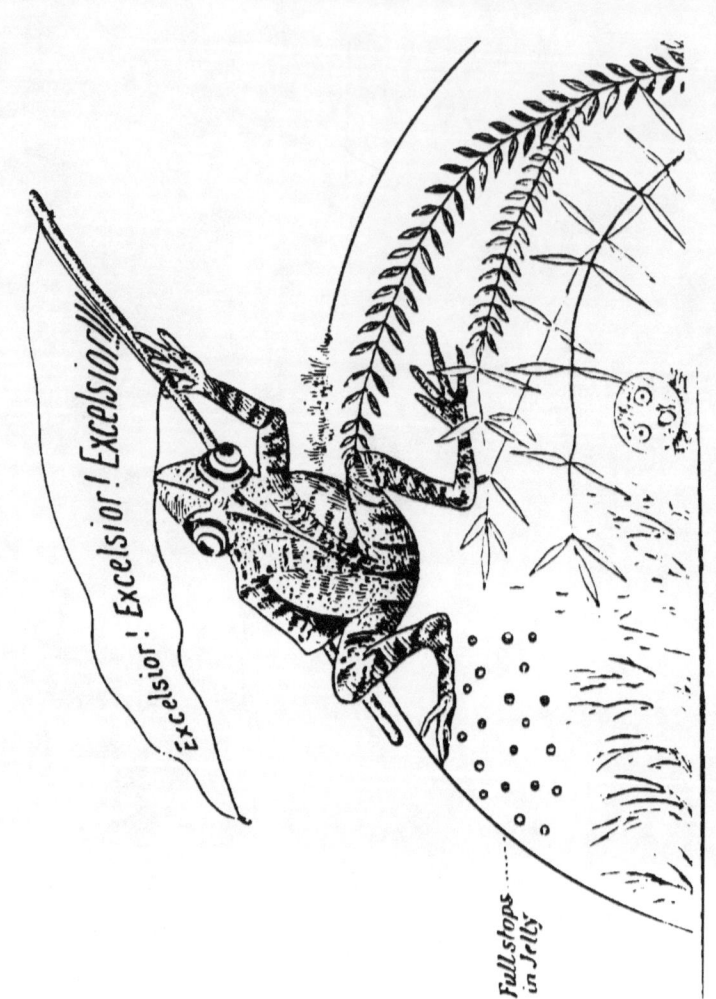

Excelsior! Excelsior! Excelsior!

Fullstops
in Jelly

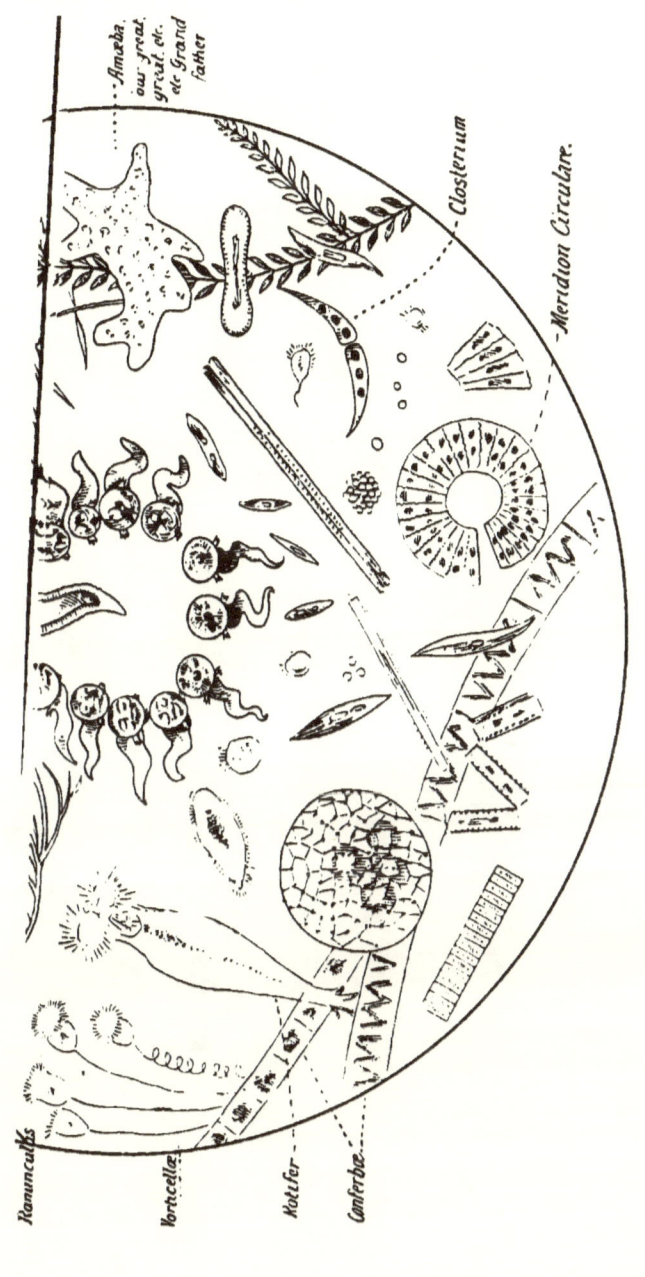

Ramunculus

Vorticellæ

Rotifer

Conferbæ

Amœba,
our great,
great, etc.
etc. Grand
father

Closterium

Meridion Circulare.

a dozen or two merry whirligig beetles frivo-
lously frisking through their usual mystic
dance on the surface, or plunging down with
silver globes on their tails to astonish and dazzle
the natives below, and a score or two of early
tadpoles. The warm sun shone in among them,
to their unmistakable enjoyment and delight,
and the surface of the water was unruffled. As I
walked home my shadow stretched before me
just ninety measured feet, a fact which will hint
to the philosophical that the sun was setting and
that I was bending my steps eastward, and which
also served to impress me with a high and mighty
sense of the importance of humanity which was
not perhaps unconnected with my subsequent
reverie. My solitary walk had been a very
happy one, and my recollection purred over it
like a gratified cat even till my bed-time; aye,
and longer too, for in my dreams I was gazing
with my binoculars into the bright waters—and
this is what I saw and heard. Under a canopy
of green callitriche a great meeting of the
"*Royal Batrachian Society*" was going on, and the
president, who was the "Tadpolean Professor of
Prehistoric Archæology," was commencing his
address on the "*Origin and Descent of Tadpole.*"
The profundity of his thoughts, the boldness of
his theories, and the inimitable vagueness of
his hypotheses are so striking that I am induced to give it without much abbreviation.

"Friends, Potladles and Polywiggles, the subject on which I desire to address you this afternoon is the all important and all absorbing one: 'The Origin and Descent of Tadpole.' Whence come we? What are we? Our past and future are alike shrouded in mystery, and their investigation is difficult and perplexing. Thanks, however, to the piercing light of modern science the mystery is not impenetrable, nor the investigation hopeless. 'What a piece of work is Tadpole' we may well exclaim with the poet; seeing that in this vast world of waters *we* undoubtedly represent the last and noblest development of organic forms —the vertebrate batrachian! Consider for a moment the exquisite beauties of our physical development;" (here the Professor expanded the broader part of his potladle); "the comeliness of our figure" (here he stretched himself to his full length or a trifle beyond it); "the elegance of our wriggle" (here his caudal extremity became spasmodic); "the vastness of our intellect; and then our Reason, which more than all elevates us above all other organisms, and begets in us an inward consciousness of superiority, and a firm conviction of a future state in which our already beautiful bodies shall become more beautified, and our mental capabilities further expanded." (At this point the Professor assumed an air of unmistakable sublimity). "But of this more anon; let us dwell at present—an agreeable task—on our own excellences and perfections. What then is beyond the reach of our enormous faculties? Doth not the Tadpole eye distinguish objects at the most remote distances, say of an inch-and-a-half radius, and in clear weather two inches? Is not its magnifying power almost unlimited, equal say to a Smith and Beck's eighth achromatic, aided by a Wenham's parabolic reflector? How else could I distinctly see the exquisite markings on that tiny Pleurosigma Formosum.* What fine names these insignificant creatures give themselves to be sure!" (at this point there was some disturbance caused by the unmannerly performances of a couple of rotifers and the unpleasant jerkings of a dozen ridiculous custard cups perched on the tops of animated corkscrews, and known under the name of vorticellæ, which necessitated police interference). "Doth not the Tadpole ear distinguish sounds at even greater distances? Doth not his god-like form—Batrachian Vertebrate as he is" (here the Professor struck an attitude) "render him capable of travelling prodigious distances—a yard or more this way or that, of soaring to the surface of our watery world, where ether alone limits our upward

---

* Married folks will learn with satisfaction from the name of this simple diatom that even in very ancient times the genders could not always agree.

investigations, or of plunging to the depths
where the vast deposits of untold ages bar our
progress, though even here the philosophic
mind finds food for contemplation, for immediately below the muddy surface we fall in with
the débris of uncouth and gigantic forms unknown to us as living since our appearance
here—now a full month ago; * and described by
our geologists under such names as Dodman-
nus, Sowbuggus, and the like; of bones of
mighty and extinct vertebrates such as Water-
rattius, Stickle-baccus, an enormous and perfect
skelton of Pussyus Domesticus; and, most
interesting of all, as I shall shortly show you,
the dried and flattened form of a true extinct
vertebrate Batrachian-Froggius Jumpaboutus.
There are distinct evidences that the present
order of things was immediately preceded by a
glacial period of almost incredible duration,
perhaps of many weeks, during which time the
physical condition of our waters, which are even
conjectured to have been solidified, were unfit
for the maintenance of such exquisite organisms
as ourselves. Indeed the absence of all traces
of fossilized Tadpoles in the deepest mud exca-
vations at present made proves (if any proof

---

* See the Professor's learned " Dissertation on the condition of things
(if any ?) in pre-mundane and ante-universian times."

Darwin said "it strikes me that all our knowledge about the structure
of the earth is very much like what an old hen would know of a hundred-
acre field, in a corner of which she is scratching."

were wanting) that the greatest triumph of natures' handiwork—*ourselves*, and particularly *my*-self, was her last and perfect effort. In the words of the poet—

> ' Her prentice han' with grubs began,
> And then she made the Tadpole oh ! '

But here comes the great and difficult question which it is my object in this lecture to elucidate. Did Nature really create Tadpole in his now perfect form, or has he passed through various stages of development, starting, say, from a contemptible monad, an imbecile polliwiggle or a filthy horse-leech, under the combined influences of natural selection, Pangenesis, survival of the fittest, and all the rest of it? Yes, my friends, it is an unpleasant fact that the *horse-leech* was our immediate ancestor.'' (Cries of Oh ! and Bosh !). ''You may cry ' Oh ! ' and also ' Bosh ! ' my friends, but the fact remains. The slow, the bloodthirsty, the unintellectual leech was our immediate progenitor, and he in his turn was developed through a line of slimy slugs and other nasty forms from the active monad, or the any-shaped amœba. I have spoken of the *active mo*nad, and I may here state by way of parenthesis that a transposition in the letters of the name may have taken place, and that from his wandering habits the word ought to be written *no*mad.'' (Somebody here called out "no *madder* than yourself"—he was immediately strangled). " Do you perceive that floating mass of bright transparent jelly studded with innumerable black dots? I consider those dots to represent so many full stops showing the boundary and limit of our powers of investigation into our past history, for when we step beyond these full stops, which in reality are precisely like the eggs in which we ourselves were inclosed" (cries of " shut up ") "we find ourselves immersed up to our third caudal vertebræ in theory and hypothesis. And when we once come to this we lose our wits. We see, admire, and fully appreciate great and magnificent effects, and yet deny the existence of a cause ; we perceive in everything the most exquisite evidences of contrivance and intelligent design, and yet stoutly deny the necessary inference of an intelligent contriver and designer. Can anything be more mad than this, my Brother Potladles? But my mind begins to wander, and a strange sensation overcomes me. Gracious Goodness ! I'm being developed ! I feel as if my tail were dropping off, and as if a couple of hind legs were beginning to protrude from my trousers pockets. A strange inclination to croak * also comes over me! Moreover here comes a frisky young eel who will infallibly

* This is a fatal warning, for to ' *Croak*' means to *die*.—

(*Johnson, or ought to be.*)

gobble us all up, naturally selecting the fittest and fattest of us, if we don't promptly ske-daddle—excuse the Americanism. I had a few more remarks to make as to our immense importance"—but the stampede had already taken place, and the fat and fit Professor himself alone fell a victim to the young eel's voracity.

Hum! thought I, his last words were—"our immense importance!" and yet he was only a tadpole. Now *I*, a *man*, made after God's own image, am—

> "'Not of the importance you suppose,'
> Replied a flea upon my nose;
> 'Be humble, learn thyself to scan,
> Know—pride was never meant for man,
> 'Tis vanity that swells thy mind.
> What! heaven and earth for *thee* designed!
> For *thee* made only! For our need,
> That more important fleas might feed!'"

Here I awoke with a vigorous rub at my aquiline; caught and cracked the impertinent quoter of Gay, and resolved to make another pilgrimage to the charming ditch at an early opportunity, and see if the tadpoles had *really* changed into frogs.

April 24*th*, 1888.

WHIST.

The game of whist, the best of sports,
Is loved by great and small,
And he who cannot play at *shorts*
Can scarcely play *at (t) all*.
So listen to my simple rhymes
While I its laws reveal ;
A little error oftentimes
Will make you *lose a deal*.
To life and whist this rule of old
Like sin to sorrow sticks,—
You seldom many *honours* hold
Without as many tricks.
And as we're taught by Mr. Hoyle
To shuffle ere we play,—
So shuffling off this mortal coil
Man's life doth pass away.
In whist and trade the partners' end
Is profit to secure,—
When one his tricks begins, his friend
Will *take them up*, be sure.
But if the partners' aim has missed
And not attained their butt,
What do they do in life and whist ?
Why generally—cut.—

Nov. 12*th.* 1846.

EPITAPH ON A SPORTSMAN.

His horses cost him many hundred pounds,
   He died of broken ribs and other shocks,
Lamented by his huntsman and his hounds,
   His life's great end fulfilled—*He caught a fox!*
                    Nov. 1844.

WILLIAM TELL.

A Poem—though you might not think so.

Says Mr. Tell to Master Tell,
   Though thou'rt a son of mine,
'Twould sure be better to hit thee
   Than spoil that "Sops o'wine." *

Says Master Tell to Mr. Tell,
   "'Tis but a Doctor Harvey!"
So Mr. Tell took aim so well,
   He knocked it Topsy-tarvey!
                   Nov. 1895.

EPITAPH ON A STILTON CHEESE.

Lamented Cheese, consumption's latest prey,
   E'en I can envy thee thy fleeting day,
For man to nothing falls and dies away.
   But thou grow'st *mighty* even in decay!

Written after my last luncheon off him, March 12th, 1845.

---

* The " Sops o' Wine " is an excellent eating apple, red throughout like
a blood orange, and with a rich vinous flavour which justifies its name.
It seems better known in East Anglia than elsewhere.

K

A VALENTINE.

What are valentines made of, made of?
What are valentines made of?
Cupids and darts and little red hearts
Are some of the things that they're made of.

What are young ladies made of, made of?
What are young ladies made of?
    Satins and sighs,
    Smiles and bright eyes,
Waltzes by Strauss, and fits of hysterics
(Cured by the cold-water cure of empirics),
    Acting charades
    And visiting cards,
Cavatinas, worked slippers, merinoes and lawns,
    A new German song
    Uncommonly long
Accompanied often by Schubert and yawns,
And little French words in little odd places
With very odd genders and very odd cases;
Mix these all together, and soon you'll see how-a-
    way's
Found out for making young ladies of now-a-
    days.
Yet in generalizing at this rate, I fear I ill
Use one who's formed of much better material.
So according to recipe (*vide* above).
I'll write a few lines to the girl that I *love*,
And endeavour to shew in each word and each line
How much I esteem my own fair Valentine :—

Dear B— ——
     How can I to you impart
An idea of the hole that you've made in my
    heart?
How can my mournful and simply-told ditty be
Tender enough to induce you to pity me?
My words seem at zero, my blood boils away
When to paint *my* true love, or *your* worth, I essay.
By Cupid's swift arrow, believe me, I *am* shot
And can no more escape than a fly in a jam pot
(A simile much less refined than convenient,
But to poets in love you must always be lenient).
It was not your form, which is not to be sneezed
    at,
Nor your face, which all eyes that have seen must
    be pleased at,
That set fire to my heart, put my nerves in a
    thrill,
But, as Moore says, "'Twas something more ex-
    quisite still."
'Twas all that is charming and pleasing, and
    more,
Or to use a French phrase,'twas a "*je ne sais quoi!*"
     If you love me as I love you
     No knife shall cut our love in two;
     If I love you let every line
     Above bear witness—
                  VALENTINE.

INQUEST ON LADY GALLINULE, OF BULL-RUSH HALL, NEAR SCOLE.

. . . . you will be interested to hear the particulars of a case which recently occurred in my practice.

Mr. C—— who was strolling about his lawn near the swamp which impinges on the land (?) of Bull-rush Hall, found this poor lady, dead and cold, lying on the grass with the nail and forefinger of her left hand thrust into, and firmly embedded in her throat; the skin of which was perforated immediately behind her chin. It seemed clear that the poor lady, whose mental balance had been disturbed, in all probability by the Anglo-Portuguese question, the influenza epidemic, or some such matter, had in a rash moment committed suicide.

The body, however, was given over to my care for further investigation, and the coroner communicated with. On the following day an inquest was held. The jury having viewed the body, the coroner (A. Gander, Esq.) said, that under the circumstances it would be unnecessary to detain them, as the case was evidently one of determined suicide, and he would ask the gentlemen of the jury to return a verdict to that effect. The Foreman having signified that it would be satisfactory to summon certain witnesses, Mr. Jeremy Jackass was called, but refused to be sworn on the ground that he was an "Atheist, and an Agnostic, don't-yer-know, and all that sort of thing! He could only say that he was thistle-browsing near the spot where the body was found, and as far as he could see (which was about one inch before his face), there was no reason to doubt that the lady died by her own hand, particularly as her finger was found in her throat.

A frog who was next put in the box " had jumped to the same conclusion." At this point the most sensible of the twelve jurymen ventured to suggest that it might be satisfactory to call the medical gentleman who had examined the body, a course which was unwillingly assented to by the Coroner, who said something about expense to the county, and luncheon time!

Dr. Drake, (don't say, 'quack, quack,') was then sworn, and gave his evidence in such admirably scientific language, that neither the Coroner, nor the jury, nor the public, nor for that matter the doctor himself could understand one word of it. It chanced however that an Interpreter was present who was familiar with Dog-Latin, Gypsey-patter, Double-Dutch,

Gibberish, and other languages, and he thus explained it. The doctor had examined the body about twelve hours after death, and had found the forefinger of the left hand firmly thrust into the windpipe through a wound which had penetrated the coverings of the neck just behind the nose. This of course looked like suicide, but on further investigation, a blood stain was found an inch and a-half further down the neck, which he at first thought had been caused by the penetration of the lady's sharp nail through the skin; on careful dissection however this turned out not to be the case, for the marks of teeth (doubtless those of a weasel), were discovered, and it was plain that the poor lady had been attacked by one of those ferocious animals, and in her struggles to dislodge him had inflicted the wound on her own throat.

The jury retired for three minutes, and then returned a verdict of "Wilful murder against some weasel or weasels unknown." Now this case is true, in all its main facts, and I ask you to consider its vast importance in a medico-legal point of view. If an arrest is effected, the defence will of course be that although the deceased had undoubtedly been attacked and wounded by the prisoner, yet there was no proof that the injury inflicted was the cause of death. On the contrary there is every reason to believe that the wound in the windpipe, indisputably

self-inflicted, was the fatal one, The evidence
of no less than twelve eminent surgeons will be
taken, six of them positively swearing one way,
and half a dozen of them the other, so that the
result is uncertain! In this state of things
we would earnestly advise that the wretched
prisoner should be hung first and tried afterwards !

See "Lynch" on the advantages of early
capital punishment in doubtful cases.

Jan. 23*rd*, 1890.

EPITAPH.

(By a Sufferer).

On . . . . . Esqre.

He paid the debt of Nature and 'tis said
This is the only debt he ever paid.

Oct. 14*th*, 1884.

At a Concert, in the Summer of 1894, our principal Singer
failed to appear.

Our Tenor cometh not, alack a-day !
The even tenor of his way diverted ;
And we who go to *concerts* here at *Diss*,
Of course you'll guess were somewhat *dis-concerted*.

1894.

MARGINAL NOTES.

The Author being an intense admirer of the "Ancient
Mariner" dareth to imitate Coleridge's notes.

The Doctor is bebothered before breakfast
by four or five patients, nevertheless he
keepeth his equanimity,
rideth out,
and wondereth when he
shall breakfast.

He is again bebothered by Miss Fozey,
Master James Slipper,
Mr. Fiddledumdee,
and Farmer Smith.
He maketh up his medicines and
muttereth aloud in dog-latin, and also
in English, his prescriptions—
—He wondereth when he shall dine.

SURGERY LYRICS, OR THE PLEASURES
OF COUNTRY PRACTICE.

Please, Sir, you're wanted to go up to Huggins's,
Three of the boys in convulsions are lying.
Then if you please after calling at Muggins's,
Mrs. Smith's sick, and the baby's a dying.
    Very well, very well, take out the physic,
    Don't lose a minute, but saddle the Bay;
    Three with the spasms, and four with the
      Phthisic!
    —Wonder what time I shall breakfast to day?

Please, Sir, Miss Fozey has got the lumbago,
And Master James Slipper has broken his nose,
May Mr. Fiddledumdee eat some sago?
And please, Sir, a mare has smashed farmer
    Smith's toes.
    Very well, very well,—Jalap, Potassa,
    Rhubarb, Hydrargyrum, Myrrh and Quinine,
    Sachari albi two drachms, fiat massa—
    —Wonder at what time I'm likely to dine!

Miss Jones is astonished!
and gently but cleverly reproveth
the Doctor for his neglect ;
seeketh information on an important point.
The Doctor *apparently* keepeth his equanimity,
and apologizeth to the ancient damsel,
giveth the required information,
but giveth vent to an unholy wish.*

A "gratis" patient sendeth
and stateth
that the Doctor's medicine
hath killed her.
The Doctor keepeth his equanimity and
moralizeth,
—Wondereth what time he shall sup.

* For which unholy wish the author wondereth that the Doctor was not doomed to wear Miss Jones round his neck. Would'st thou rather be the Doctor with a Miss Jones, or an Ancient Mariner with an albatross? Echo answereth—With an albatross!!!

Please, Sir, Miss Jones is surprised you've not
    been to her,
Says, she supposed that you must have been ill;
Thought that *if not*, you would *surely* have seen
    to her ;
Wants to know how she's to swallow the pill.

    Very well, very well, tell her my sorrow,
    Say it was far from my wish to provoke her,
    The pill in some jam, and I'll call in
        to-morrow,
    Drat the old woman, I wish it may choke her.

Please, Sir, the woman you physic for nothing
Has just sent up word by her daughter Matilda,
And says that all day she's been gasping and
    puffing,
And please Sir, she thinks that your mixture has
    killed her.

    Very well, very well, that they call gratitude.
    Tell the poor girl that I'll shortly step up.
    Charity! wide as the world is thy latitude!
     Wonder what time of the night I shall sup!

The doctor
is awakened from his first sleep
and hath the prospect
of a delightful journey,
But he keepeth his equanimity
and yet he wondereth
if Job was a country doctor,
and *if so* draweth a conclusion.

The author sweareth
that nothing is exaggerated, and
signeth himself
A Member of the Royal College of Surgeons.

He kindly prescribeth
for his Reader.

Please, Sir, you've got to get up and to ride
Just past the sixth milestone on Slobberwash
   Moor,
For old Squire Grunt has a pain in his side,
And his man's got a lantern and horse at the
   door.
   Very well, very well, bed was just warming ;
   Snow, too, and sleet from a pitchy black sky.
   If Job practised physic without ever storming,
   Shoot *me* if he hadn't more patience than I!

Oh doubt me not, reader- I've said what the
   fact is,
I've given no overdrawn case of distress,
But merely set down what I've oft seen in
   practice ;
All this do I swear to!—Signed—M.R.C.S.

   Senna, Lythargyrum, oil of sweet marjoram,
   Pulvis emeticus, Haustus sudaticus,
   Sumbul with foxy smell, syrup and oxymel,
   Wondrous dispensing by prentice commencing!

   Gentle reader, if thine eyes are red with weeping at our hard lot- allow me to prescribe for
thee !

     The Eye Water to be used
        frequently.

                 1847.

THE SONG OF THE PILL.

With face so weary and worn,
With eyelids heavy and red,
A "Doctor" sat in his shabby old coat
Making a bolus of bread.
    Mix, pill, mix,
With rhubarb, magnesia, and squill.
And still with a voice of dolorous pitch
He sang this song of the pill.

    Ride, ride, ride,
Ere the cock is crowing aloof;
    And mix, mix, mix,
Till the fumes mount up to the roof.
Ointment, powder, and draught.
Gentian, soda, and squill,
Making at once for your patient's use
A shroud as well as a pill.

    Stir, stir, stir,
Till the mortar begins to spin;
    And mix, mix, mix,
Till all's forgotten that's in;
Zinc and alum and tar,
Journeys, attendance, and craft,
Till over the lotion I fall asleep,
And send it out as a draught

Called out to cure a cold * - (Jan.\ 20.\ 2 o'clock A.M. 6 Mile ride)

*"The Patient", not the Doctor

Oh! man with fancies and gout,
Oh, maids with pains in the head,
They are not pills that you're taking there,
But little knubbles of bread.
    Ride, ride, ride,
In swamp, in shower, and dirt,
Damping at once to the innermost thread
The spirits as well as the shirt.

O! but to sit for an hour
With feet tucked under the grate
Where never a night bell's sound was heard,
When the pillow has eased one's pate;
For only one short day
To feel as I used to feel,
Ere yet I had made ten patients away
Or choked myself with my meal.

With face so weary and worn,
With eyelids heavy and red,
A parish "Doctor" gloomily sat
Making a bolus of bread.
    Mix, pill, mix,
For all the paupers are ill,
And still with a voice of an ill-paid tone
(Would that the guardians had heard the moan)
    He sang the "Song of the Pill."

March 25th, 1849.

BRITISH BULL DOGS AND KILKENNY CATS.

The dogs and the cats lived a cat-and-dog life,
For the dogs laid down the laws ;
They were bull dogs of fighting British blood,
Knowing nothing of cattish ways ;
And the cats were the famed Kikenny* brood,
Which scratch for scratch repays :
So pussy's compliance was spits and defiance,
With liberal use of her claws.
Such howlings and growlings, and swearing, and
　　strife,
Mr. Mallock would say "not worth living" such life !
But a wise old Feller was passing by,
With his axe, and his collars up ever so high ;
He was thinking of Ireland's troubles and woes,
And his thoughts got a little mixed up, I suppose ;
For he said, said he, this must not be
'Tis idle to look for content and repose
While A snarles at B, and B scratches A's nose :
So away with your dog legislation ;
Let puss make her laws for her kits and herself,
Put malice and hate high away on the shelf,
While you defend all with your arms and your
　　pelf.
Then, if Justice and Mercy go hand in hand,
You'll settle your questions of tenants and land,
A united and happy nation.

* Let them govern themselves in both senses, and show men, the tale
of the tails is a myth. *Absit omen*.

HIGH CLASS (A1) BOTANY.

About to be published in the new series of " Papers for Thoughtful Girls."

Question 1. What is the origin of the term *Endogenous*?

Answer. As Adam and Eve were walking together in the garden the former nudged the latter, and spying the serpent in the tree of knowledge, whispered—"I say Eve, there's N . . . (meaning Nick) dogin' us. Eve always after called it the "N-dogin-us tree."

Q. 2. What is a boot tree?

A. 2. A member of the *shu-mac* family.

Q. 3. Now describe a Whipple-tree.

A. 3. It is closely connected to the Horse-tails (Equisetaceæ).

Q. 4. What is your opinion respecting Jack's Bean-stalk?

A. 4. That it was not a *bean* at all—the name 'Faba' being probably a corruption of the word '*Fable.*' Its climbing stem must have been composed of an infinite number of 'Scalariform' (ladder-like) vessels growing end to end (so as to enable its proprietor to ascend to an enormous height) and of a few *cells*, the biggest of which fell to the lot of Jack's parents when they found he had bartered their valuable cow for it's worthless seed.

Q. 5. Of what use is the Pisum Maritimum?

A. 5. To make Pea-jackets for Mariners, I suppose.

Q. 6. What plant is alluded to in the following beautiful verse—

"It grew and it grew till it reached the church top,
　It grew and it grew much higher,
And it twined itself into a true loveyer's knot,
　All true loveyers for to admire."

A. 6. Most likely a clematis, which only means a "climber-'tis."

Q. 7. What did Shakespeare mean by finding—"Tongues in trees, and books in the running brooks"?

A. 7. It is all a mistake. In my Folio of sixteen hundred and odd, the "old common tater" has it correctly—thus—"Finds *books* in trees"—doubtless alluding to the *liber* which underlies the outer bark. As for the "Tongues in the running brooks" you must of course look for them in the *mouth* of the stream.

Q. 8. What is a Radicle—

A. 8. Oh! if you're going to talk politics, teacher, I shut up—for I'll have nothing to say to your Radicals. -Not I!!!

　　　　　Finis, in a huff!

Very Many Thanks for all those delicious
Candied Dates. There were 3 candidates

All Hot!
for mince pies a day,
a py mince pies a day,

off the Candy and left the 2 dates!!

Those dates were 1886 and 1887, which

reminds me to wish you a very happy

New Year.

. If you don't quite understand this note,

(and I can't say I do) ask papa to lend you

his razor-strap to sharpen your wits on.

Believe Me Dear Mary,

Your very affectionate old Doctor

Prose Versifications and Translations.

THE YOUNG MARINE AT HANGO-HEAD.

(See the letter extracted from the *Boston Guardian* of
July 5th, 1854).

We landed on the Finnish shore
  And straggled from our boat,
To guard our seamen while they took
  The battery's guns afloat.

From out a copse the Russians stole,
  I marked my man full well,
Took steady aim—a moment passed
  And like a stone he fell.

A broadside from our frigate then
  Flew thick among the wood,
And where they went God knows, but none
  Were standing where they stood.

L 2

And where was now my enemy ?
  A strange resistless force
Drew me to *him*, and savage hate
  Was changed to deep remorse.

Oh ! 'twas a feeling dread and new
  Even in mortal strife,
That I with vengeful hand could take
  A fellow-creature's life !

Far more I feared the bleeding form
  That stretched before me lay,
Than the young soldier who but now
  Full eager, sought the fray.

I dropped beside him on my knees,
  My heart seemed flowing o'er,
And tears gushed freely from my eyes
  As ne'er they gushed before.

He looked not like a foeman now,
  And with a comrade's eye
I marked his pale but manly brow,
  And heaved a brother's sigh.

He grasped my hand ; thank God, he saw
  No spot of murderous red,
But in its place a stainless drop,
  In truest sorrow shed.

He pointed where his comrades lurked,
  He pointed to the shore,
And seemed to say, "now save thyself,"
  But uttered nought but gore.

A gun was fired from our ship
  To call her scattered crew,
And ere its thunder-roll had ceased
  His spirit upward flew.

O, could I with my life have bought
  The life I'd snatched away,
Full willingly I then had sought
  My blood for *his* to pay.

With thoughts of fame and victory
  I tried my heart to cheer ;
But these all seemed so far away
  And the dead man so near!

Almighty God ! I humbly pray
  That (all my sins forgiven)
We yet may meet when strife is o'er
  As faithful friends in Heaven.

          30th July, 1854.

ALABASTER BOXES OF HUMAN SYMPATHY.

Versified from a passage by an unknown Author.

Keep not your stores of love and tenderness
In alabaster boxes closely sealed
Until your friends are dead, but fill their lives
With sweetness; speak approving, cheering
    words
While yet their ears can hear them; while their
    hearts
Can yet be thrilled by them, and happier made.
The kind and loving things you mean to say
When they are gone, say now before they go.
The flowers you mean to strew their coffins with
Send now to sweeten and adorn their homes
Before they leave them. If my friends possess
In Alabaster boxes laid away
Rich perfumes of warm sympathy and love
Which they intend when I am dead to break
Over my senseless body—I would say,
Open them now, and with their sweetness cheer
My weary, troubled hours, while yet I live.
Rather a coffin without wreath or flower,
A stone without an epitaph, than life
Without the sweetness of abiding love.
Let us anoint our friends before they leave
For their long journey hence. Remember this
Love after death can cheer no burdened mind,
And flowers on the coffin cast no charm,
No fragrance backward on the weary way.

EVOLUTION.

"There is a natural body, and there is a spiritual body.
. . . . . Howbeit, that was not first which is spiritual, but
that which is natural, and afterward that which is spiritual."

Let your imagination do its best
To summon up the past of glorious nature ;
The mystic panorama of its birth
In starry nebulæ : some specks of which
Conjoined, consolidated, formed our earth
With oceans interspersed and lights to rule
The night and cheerful day ; then run the eye
Through Æons past, when simple living things
Begat dread monsters whose gigantic forms,
Unknown to man, lie buried in the rocks,
With plants and trees all strange and wonderful.
Watch the majestic drama, scene by scene,
And act by act, unfolding.   Realize
That one great Power, and one great Power alone,
Has marshalled in this mighty spectacle
With all its varied figures; One Great Hand
Has carried out their transformations; One
And one alone high Principle controlled
Each plot and circumstance.   The same great
    Law

Patient and unobtrusive shaped the whole
From its beginnings in bewilderment
And dreary chaos, to its glorious End
In order, harmony, and perfect beauty.
Then watch the curtain drop, and as it moves
To rise again—behold upon the stage
Another actor?—silently and still,
As all great changes come, it takes its place
As *Mental Evolution*, and succeeds
Organic Progress, which must henceforth lie
In the far background with forgotten things.
Man, in the foreground stands erect,—and lo!
A new thing—*God's own Spirit*—strives within
    him.

        Versified from Drummond's " Ascent of Man," end of
          Chapter III. (Diss, Oct. 15*th*, 1894.)

HEAVEN.

A land of beauty For myself I love
To fancy heaven much like our present earth,
But free from imperfections. If we reach,
Or let me rather phrase it—*When* we reach
That country, it will be in glorious form -
Yet in the body, purified and clean.
Almighty God, who made the earth for man,

Body and soul, pronounced it " very good;"
Nor can I in my fancy conjure up
A place more fitted for man's happiness
(If we were only sinless, loving God,
And in God loving too his fellow man)
Than this same earth.   And God too has prepared
Man's home in heaven, will He not pronounce
It also " very good"?   We Christian men
Might long for Heaven more truly, and might
    strive
With firmer resolution to attain
Its great reward, if we at once put off
The childish notion, got I know not how,
Of flying in the air, with nought to do
But singing songs of praise, like human birds.
Why not suppose that all that's bright and pure,
All that delights and makes us happy here,
Music and learning, art, and trees, and flowers,
The joys of home, sweet converse with our
    friends,
All that is innocent and fair and good
Will be the promised, perfect bliss of heaven?

Versified from Blakelock's " Coming to Christ."   1892.

(The Idea from Fontenelle's "Entretiens sur la pluralité
des mondes.")

Each blooming rose left record of its fleeting
    summer day
Ere twilight stole the fragrance from its fallen
    flower away.
And the first rose in the garden praised the
    wisdom and the care
Of the good and skilful gardener who had trained
    her branches there.
Nay more, had left his portrait and described his
    person too,
And the picture and description both were of the
    roses' hue.
Ten thousand roses' ages now have passed away
    and gone,
Yet the portrait and its history to each fragile
    flower are known,
And thus they say "'tis clear that in the
    memory of the rose,
Saving a furrow here, this face no alteration
    knows.
Our gardener is immortal then, for as of old we
    see
His form to-day, and doubtless thus it evermore
    shall be!"

* De mémoire de Rose on n'a point vu mourir le Jardinier.

Oh man, whose life is as the rose, whose little
    day is spent
In the record of thy story—dost thou watch the
    firmament?
Dost view the countless suns above with con-
    templative eye
And say—"All men shall perish, but behold
    eternity?"
Forget not that a Pleiad's gone, that stars which
    once were bright
E'en in our father's memory have vanished from
    our sight.
So thoughtful men and roses in their short and
    fleeting day
May in the stars and gardener too—find traces
    of decay.

Diss, June 9th, 1862.

These ideas are taken from various authors.

The dim and bounded intellect of man
Doth rarely prosper when it seeks to scan
And dogmatize on matters infinite;
Vast and minute alike elude his sight,

(Boyle.)

Who, his Creator's ways would well discern
Must to great Nature's sacred temple turn
Bible in hand,—and meekly wisdom learn.

(French of Gaede.)

In the still hours of Life man's talent forms,
His *Character* shoots forth amid its storms.

(Goethe.)

To know our God is learning's noble end,
And then our knowledge in His love to spend;
And this we may attain the nearest way
By seeking virtue's footsteps day by day.

(Milton's prose.)

There is a knowledge which creates a doubt,
And nought but larger knowledge helps it out;
The man who, faltering, stops in middle way
Perplexed and troubled meets his dying day.

(Sharon Turner.)

Our great philosophers do easily
Bear sorrows past, or sorrows yet to be,
But *present* woes do vex them grievously.

(La Rochefoucauld.)

Men, for the most part, rarely silence break
When vanity bestirs them not to speak,
And some prefer themselves ill names to call
To never speaking of themselves at all.

(Idem.)

Mere contact with fair Nature issuing forth
Into the free and open air, doth give
A soothing sense of calmness to the heart,
And still the boisterous passions of mankind.
'Tis felt by all—no matter of what clime,
Or what degree of culture we enjoy.
That which is grave and solemn is derived
From the presentiment of ruling law,
Of perfect order, and supreme control,
Which simple outward nature doth inspire.
—It is derived too from a contrast made
Between our finite being and the sense
Of vast infinity, which everywhere
Doth press upon our thoughts, when we regard
The starry depths of Heaven,—the boundless
　　plain,
Or ocean's blue horizon, dimly seen.
　　　　　　　　　　　　　(*Humboldt's Cosmos*).

The saddest tears shed over graves are those
Which fall for words unsaid, and deeds undone;
"She never knew I loved her so," or "he
Knew not how much he was to me," and yet
I always meant while he was with us here
To make more of his friendship; oh 'tis strange
How little I suspected—'till he died,
The pang of losing him. Too late! too late!"
Such thoughts are poisoned arrows which grim
　　death
Shoots backward at us from the silent tomb.
　　　　　　(*Mrs. H. B. Stowe's "Little Foxes."*)

Faith, Hope, and Love! and of these three the
    greatest, Love, we prize ;
For Faith and Hope are but the wings which
    Love the Seraph plies.

             (" *Life Thoughts.*")

As birds in transmigration feel the charm
Of southern lands, and gladly spread their wings
T'wards the bright realms of light and bloom—
    so we
In the dark hour of death may feel with joy
Solicitations of the life beyond;
And from the chilly shadow of the earth
Soar high, and singing fold our wings to rest
In the bright summer of eternal heaven.

             (*Ibid.*)

I've seen luxuriant grasses growing up
E'en from the tops of graves; and sweetest
    flowers
Bursting from out the crevices of tombs.—
And then I've thought of the fair life of those
Who, born in sin, and sinning in their youth,
Have found the error of their ways, and walked
In the sweet paths of virtue -for the corpse
With its corruptions and its wasting flesh
Lay 'neath the fragrant flowers.--Yet ere long
That corpse shall perish with its crumbled tomb,
And nought shall mark its place but fruitful
    bloom.

        (*Idea partly from* " *Life Thoughts.*")

Love, in this world, is like a precious seed
Brought from the sunny south, and planted here
Where winter comes too soon.   It cannot spread
In flower clusters and wide-twining vines,
So that the world may taste its sweet perfume.
But there will be another summer yet!
Care for the root then, nurse it tenderly,
And God will bid it blossom by and bye.

(Ibid.)

We ought to love our life, and to desire
To live as long as God shall deem it well.
But let us not encase ourselves in time
So firmly that we cannot break its crust,
And throw our shoots out for the other life.

(Ibid.)

Time guides our hands, and aided thus we write
Our Journals day by day,—and they are true;
The falsest one among us nought but truth
Can enter on these pages—nought omit,
Nought soften, or disguise.   Oh God, do thou
Temper Thy justice with a Father's love
When Thou shalt read my life's sad history.

(Ibid.)

When Love is in the heart, then in the eyes
Are rainbows, gilding with their gorgeous dyes
The murky clouds that ever threatening rise.

(Ibid.)

Unloving words are meant to make us kind,
Delays teach patience, and care fosters faith;
While press of business makes us look for time
To give to God, and disappointed hopes
Are special messengers to mortals given,
Calling our thoughts from earth, to rest in
    Heaven.

                          (*Elizabeth M. Sewell.*)

TRANSLATION FROM HORACE. ODE XXII. LIB. I.

"AD ARISTIUM FUSCUM." "INTEGER VITÆ."

He that is pure of heart and knows no guiling
Needs neither Moorish javelins, nor the bow;
Useless to him were sheaves of poisoned arrows
                Loading his quiver;

Whether his way o'er Lybian desert wending,
Or frozen Caucasus' unfriendly snows,
Or by thy dark and sable-teeming waters,
                Golden Hydaspes.

NOTE.—My brother wanting English words to "Integer vitae" to print opposite the Latin ones of Fleming's exquisite part song, we both set to work. My attempt is above. It was my aim to translate as literally as possible, and above all to preserve the metre with its rhymeless lines generally ending with a dissyllabic word.

Lately in Sabine woods my footsteps straying,
Singing of Lalage, I knew not whither,
Swiftly a wolf fled from me, greatly fearing
          Me all unarméd.

Raging and gaunt, no brute more fierce and cruel
Fell Daunias nourished in her beechen groves,
Nor Juba, arid nurse of hungry lions
          Savagely roaring.

Place me where never graceful branches waving
Play in the breathings of the sunlit air,
Or where the lurid clouds descend in tempest
          Jupiter ruling:

Place me beneath the sun's intemperate burning,
On scorching plains, where men ne'er make their
    dwelling;
Still will I love my Lalage, my darling,
          Lalage smiling.
                Nov. 14*th*, 1884.

M

"INTEGER VITÆ."

(CHRISTIAN FORM).

He that is pure and hateth all things evil
Needs not with mail his honest strength en-
cumber,
Needs not the deadly sword or shining buckler's
Breadth to protect him;

Whether in wilds where savage wolves are
howling,
Or gloomy haunts where fiercer brigands linger,
Or on the field by battle-strife ensanguined
Fearless he wanders.

Once roaming free by rock and frowning forest
Wolf-like the tempter dogged my careless stray-
ing,
Straightway I raised my song of praise, and
Satan
Trembled and fled me.

Place me mid terrors—thrust me 'mong the lions,
Let murderous steel my fragile body sever,
Yet still my Soul shall sing in praise unceasing
God my Creator:

Place me in scorching heat, in withering cold-
   ness,
Cast me on ocean's never-resting waters
Still shall my Spirit laud my Sweet Redeemer
           Jesus my Saviour.

Yet leave me not alone thou Spirit Holy,
For I am weak, unaided by Thy power;
Dwell in me, Lord, thou Comforter Almighty,
          So I am fearless.   *
                  Nov. 18th, 1884.

DEDICATION TO FAUST.

(*Goethe*).

Unfixed and faltering forms, you come again,
You that long since my troubled sight did greet;
Do I yet seek your misty shapes to gain?
Leans yet my heart to some unknown conceit?
You still approach—then unresisted reign,
As ye in mist and cloud around me meet.
My bosom, as in youth, heaves once again
With magic breath that trembles round your
   train.

M 2

The forms of other days you lead along,
And many a well-loved shadow rises near
Like to an old and half-forgotten song.
First love and friendship hand in hand appear;
Pain comes anew, bewailing every wrong
Of life's confused and many changing year,
And names the good who of the cheerful light
By fate deprived, have vanished from my sight.

You cannot now the following numbers hear,
You who long since received my early lay;
No more I see the friends who once were dear;
My song's first echo now has died away.
To unknown multitudes my lays appear,
Whose very praises my sad heart dismay;
And they who first delighted in my song
Wander—if living—distant lands among.

Once more a long forgotten wish I feel
Pensive to tread the Spirit's magic ground,
As soft th' Æolean harp's sweet murmurs steal,
So half expressed my numbers hover round.
I tremble, and in vain my tears conceal,
Now to soft feeling yields my heart's firm
    bound,
What I behold, illusive seems to be,
And what is not, appears reality.

Sept. 2nd, 1842.

THE SUN-DIAL.

" Horas non numero nisi serenas."—*Old Motto.*

I count the hours by joyous sunshine made,
The rest lie unrecorded in the shade.

June, 1878.

———

THE WEST.

From the German of Matthisson.

Golden beams
Light the streams,
Falling as with magic power
O'er the ruin'd forest-tower.

Broad and free
Glows the sea;
Soft as swans, and gently riding,
Fisher's boats are homeward gliding.

Silver sand
Decks the strand:
Ruddy clouds in ceaseless motion
Throw their changing forms on ocean

Crimson'd o'er;
Near the shore
Sighing rushes fringe the crest,
Where the seabird builds her nest.

Deep in shade
Down the glade,
Where the mossy springs are swelling,
Lies the hermit's peaceful dwelling.

Latest day
Dies away,
Palely fades the twilight hour
Glimmering on the ruin'd tower.

Full moonlight
Cheers the night,
Spirit voices sweep the vales
Whispering bygone battle tales.

Dec. 5th, 1840.

SOLDIER'S MORNING SONG.

Translated from German, "Soldaten Lieder."

Dawn of day, dawn of day,
Points to death thy crimson ray?
Soon the trumpets wildly braying
Rolling drums and chargers neighing
Shall to battle call away.

Ere 'tis known, ere 'tis known
Pleasure's sweetest hour has flown ;
Now the war-horse proudly training—
Next the heart's-blood earthward draining—
    Then the cold and silent tomb.

Short the time, short the time,
    Beauty's pride and youthful prime;
Lilies fair with rose buds blending,
Every charm so vainly lending,—
    Ah! the roses fall and die.

Who shall know, who shall know
Pleasure's fulness here below ?
Hearts with care and sorrow aching,
E'en from morning's early breaking
    Till the western fires glow.

Let me still, let me still
    Bow to God's resistless will ;
Firm in Heaven's help relying
Fearless live, or fearless dying
    As a Christian soldier still.

Aug. 26th, 1855.

AN EPIGRAM.

Translated from the French.

Damon loves but himself;
All his choice must approve,
For he'll ne'er know the pain
Of a rival in love.

WORDS TO THE GERMAN AIR "AN DEN MOND."

The first stanza is freely translated from the German.

Gentle moon, so calmly sailing
    In the glittering evening sky,
My sad heart in sighs and wailing
    Marks thy peaceful course on high.
Tears are falling,—while I ponder
    On thy still and holy flight
And my soul in speechless wonder
    Longs with thee to share the night.
Neither gold nor earthly treasure
    Can thy heavenly course impede,
Nor the wiles of guilty pleasure
    From thy path of glory lead.
Oh in pity—far from sadness
    Take, oh take me now with thee,
And in Angel-worlds of gladness
    Let our place of resting be.

                        June 14th, 1854.

SONG.

From the German.

Far away----from bygone day—
From youth's fair springtime gleaming,
In joy or pain there comes again
A form with brightness beaming.
Full well I know the lips' warm glow
That whispering used to greet me;
The brow so fair, the golden hair,
The cheek that flushed to meet me.
For though the strife of warring life
May cloud its youthful morning,
Touched by its magic yet
Ne'er can the heart forget
Its dream of love's first dawning.

Past the glow of burning day,
And stars in heaven are smiling,
Onward still it cheers my way,
The tedious hours beguiling.
The livelong night by watchfires light
I lay, and still 'twas nigh me,
I crossed the free and foaming sea,
And at the helm 'twas by me.
For though the strife of warring life

May cloud its youthful morning,
Touched by its magic yet
Ne'er can the heart forget
Its dream of love's first dawning.

Like a wild and artless child
With smiles through tear-drops glowing,
With playful air its golden hair
About my shoulder throwing,—
Such bliss it brings—so sweetly sings
In tones of joy or sadness
That gushing tears bring boyhood's years
With all their sunny gladness.
—For though the strife of warring life
May cloud its youthful morning,
Lulled by its memory yet
Ne'er can the heart forget
Its dream of love's first dawning.—

Feb. 7th, 1857.

Acrostics and Charades, &c.

I.

DOUBLE ACROSTIC.

With one small hint my first and last you'll guess,
To throw my last on first is vain excess.

1. Beneath your feet, yet not upon the ground.
2. Valued in summer, but in winter found.
3. Dividing streams, and rising with a feather.
4. Two pages I, placed dos à dos together.
5. Frenchmen discern me in each babbling rill.
6. In Oxford I was hung, and hang there still.
7. Most folks get over me, yet I'm not weak,
   But were I so they'd chance their shins to
      break.

2.

A DOUBLE ACROSTIC.

1. What a hare is when 'tis roasted, what a sole
   is when 'tis fried,
   What a rotten bank's accounts are, with a lot
   of things beside ;
2. Next a famed Italian poet shall his kind
   assistance lend,
3. And a thing that tight-laced people are
   familiar with, to end.   ·
   If you put these well together in due order,
   there shall come
   Two friends of ours, not seldom to be seen
   about our home.

3.

C H A R A D E .

Beneath my *third* my *first* is tied,
And that which goes between,
In every hut, in every house
Save our own home, is seen.
My *whole* doth well corroborate
The truth of Darwin's plan,
As more than half a monkey,
Though undoubtedly a man !

4.

CHARADE.

My *first* 'twixt earth and sky is laid ;
My *second* out of clay is made :
My *first* and *second* joined, though brave, would
    very useless be
Without my *third*, or having that I can't
    exactly see
Their use without my *whole*—or if possessive he
    should prove
Why then without my *third*, aloft, he'd very
    slowly move.

Nov. 18th, 1882.

5.

A CHARADE.

Without my *first* this beauteous world would
    seem
A dreary chaos ; sun and stars would move
In wild disorder: Athens and queenly Rome
Had been unbuilt: man's nature purposeless ;
And beauty's symmetry and form unknown.
My *second's* found on every noble page
Of Virgil, and 'tis more than doubtful whether
Without it he'd have strung ten lines together.
And what's my *whole*? In heaven my form you
    view,
Or you may feel me underneath your shoe.
Tell us my name or own yourself a dunce,
My very name I've placed before you once.

6.

CHARADE.

My *first* is foremost, that's perhaps no wonder!
It rolls along a ton of chattels under.
My *last* (two parts combined) will ever be
Found in each city t'other side the sea.
My *whole*, I hope you have not, yet I'm told
Not having it you're scarce of mortal mould.
What is it? All and nothing! so the sages
Say, and have said now, and in bygone ages:
Look to your every thought and deed—nor
    doubt it,
For scarce one human act is done without it:
Avoid it, hate it; 'tis the stubborn girth
That separates pure heaven from sinful earth.

Dec. 16*th.* 1875.

7.

ENIGMA.

I can't be one, and yet I'm one of five
Much prized in England. And as I'm alive
I'm hardly two, but yet I'm four, six, ten,
And thousands more, made up of living men,
Pigs, monkeys, sheep, or any mortal thing
That swims the deep, or cleaves with rapid wing
The sunny air, or to the earth doth cling.
Cut three joints from my tail, I am not dead,
But senseless as a herring, one that's red ;
Restore me two of them, and if you're clever
You'll find you've made me rather worse than
     ever.
Cut off my head and tail, and watch my hue,
'Tis neither white nor yellow, pink, nor blue.
Breathe on me while thus clipped. Behold in me
A stately river flowing to the sea.

Nov. 20th. 1871.

8.

AN ENIGMA.

I am *me* when at your house, you're *me* when at
     mine,
And my riddle's *me* too, if in riddles you shine.

Nov., 1871

9.

ENIGMA.

I'm not myself when morn is fresh and bright
Though sure to be myself before 'tis night :
And when I'm at myself I hope you'll see
The mould of fashion and of form in me.
The helmsman's wheel without being me may
    guide,
And fortune's in its airy circles glide,
But Father Time's upon the rugged road
Of the rough world would spill his weary load
Unless myself. And you too must be me,
Fair reader. Yet if fair I'm not myself of thee.

                      Nov. 20th, 1871.

———

10.

ENIGMA.

Wise I am not, and yet the learned Greek
Made me of Wisdom's self the topmost peak ;
But though the peak, should I my head embrace
Between my next and third reversed, no trace
Of pride were mine, but in me you would know
A something which you'd deem debased or low.
Restore my pristine form. If this you do
You'll think my loneliness unapt to woo

And little prone to wit ; and yet to both
When darkness veils the sky I'm nothing loth :
And if in naming me you sigh, my plight
Shall in the watch-dog's wail alarm the night;
Yet sigh no more, but from my body rip
Its double centre, now within thy grip
Thou hold'st a genesis to aid my rhyme,
The double head and dawning of Old Time.

Nov. 1871.

II.

AN ENIGMA.

I span the bridge, crowning with golden bow
A Greek or Roman hill ; sometimes beneath
A point looks heavenwards ; and deeper still
Two tunnels run to dark unknown abyss.
Often from cataract to cataract
I stretch my shining arc, at each extreme
Enclosing with a zone a crystal plain.
I am no orator, yet hold the ears
Of mighty statesmen, and I render plain
The words of Holy Writ, or Shakespeare's page,
To countless thousands who unhelped by me,
Spite of all comments, must in darkness be.

N

12.

ENIGMA.

If you call him a liar, without any doubt
You're greatly to blame, for he's not one.
Yet I freely confess you're not very much out,
Though if fishing for facts—you've not got one.
He runs, though not fast, from the East to the
    West,
And anon from the North to the South.
Icy cold—seething hot is the breath of his mouth,
So say those who full near him have pressed.
He is tall and wears spurs, he's a chain—not of
    gold—
Like the one that adorns your fair wife,
And he's longer than that, and remarkably old,
Yes, as old as the hills—'pon my life!
You're attached to the world with its sin-tainted
    leaven,
Though aspiring upward I grant you are.
So attached is our friend, and yet nearer to
    heaven
Than his Grace the Archbishop of Cantuar!

Dec. 31*st*, 1872.

ANSWERS TO ACROSTICS, &c.

1. Violets——Perfume.
    1. VamP.
    2. IcE.
    3. OaK.
    4. LeaF.
    5. EaU.
    6. ToM.
    7. StilE.

2. Cat——Dog.
    1. CookeD.
    2. AriostO.
    3. TaG.

CHARADES.	ENIGMAS.
3. Capuchin.	7. Numbers.
4. Seamanship.	8. A Guest.
5. Plan-et Tellus.	9. Tired.
6. Vanity.	10. Owl.
	11. Spectacles.
	12. Himalaya.

INDEX.

PSALMS.

BALLADS.

HEROIC.

HUMOROUS.

PROSE VERSIFICATIONS AND TRANSLATIONS.

AGAS H DOOSE, PRINTER, NORWICH.

www.ingramcontent.com/pod-product-compliance
Lightning Source LLC
Chambersburg PA
CBHW020620030726
47497CB00007B/2329